The chopper carrying Frank and Joe landed on the deck of the floating rig. Just as it touched down, an ear-splitting siren went off.

"RED ALERT!" bellowed a voice from an unseen loudspeaker. "This is not a drill! Choppers evacuate helipads! All hands report immediately to duty hazard positions!"

Frank stumbled down the steps of the helicopter, with Joe close behind. At their backs, one of the pilots slammed the hatch shut. Frank and Joe ducked as the Chinook's rotors fired up, beating the air over their heads. "Hey!" Joe yelled. "What's that?"

"What's what?" Frank turned toward his brother as the huge chopper began to lift off. Frank's heart skipped a beat when he saw what was wrong. The end of Joe's long duster coat had been caught in the helicopter's door!

"Joe!" Frank screamed as Joe yanked on his duster, trying to pull himself loose. It was too late. As Joe kicked his feet wildly, the Chinook rose from the pad, dragging its helpless passenger into the air.

## Books in THE HARDY BOYS CASEFILES™ Series

#1 DEAD ON TARGET
#2 EVIL, INC.
#3 CULT OF CRIME
#4 THE LAZARUS PLOT
#5 EDGE OF DESTRUCTION
#6 THE CROWNING TERROR
#7 DEATHGAME
#8 SEE NO EVIL
#9 THE GENIUS THIEVES
#10 HOSTAGES OF HATE
#11 BROTHER AGAINST BROTHER
#12 PERFECT GETAWAY
#13 THE BORGIA DAGGER
#14 TOO MANY TRAITORS
#15 BLOOD RELATIONS
#16 LINE OF FIRE
#17 THE NUMBER FILE
#18 A KILLING IN THE MARKET
#19 NIGHTMARE IN ANGEL CITY
#20 WITNESS TO MURDER
#21 STREET SPIES
#22 DOUBLE EXPOSURE
#23 DISASTER FOR HIRE
#24 SCENE OF THE CRIME
#25 THE BORDERLINE CASE
#26 TROUBLE IN THE PIPELINE
#27 NOWHERE TO RUN
#28 COUNTDOWN TO TERROR
#29 THICK AS THIEVES
#30 THE DEADLIEST DARE
#31 WITHOUT A TRACE
#32 BLOOD MONEY
#33 COLLISION COURSE

#34 FINAL CUT
#35 THE DEAD SEASON
#36 RUNNING ON EMPTY
#37 DANGER ZONE
#38 DIPLOMATIC DECEIT
#39 FLESH AND BLOOD
#40 FRIGHT WAVE
#41 HIGHWAY ROBBERY
#42 THE LAST LAUGH
#43 STRATEGIC MOVES
#44 CASTLE FEAR
#45 IN SELF-DEFENSE
#46 FOUL PLAY
#47 FLIGHT INTO DANGER
#48 ROCK 'N' REVENGE
#49 DIRTY DEEDS
#50 POWER PLAY
#51 CHOKE HOLD
#52 UNCIVIL WAR
#53 WEB OF HORROR
#54 DEEP TROUBLE
#55 BEYOND THE LAW
#56 HEIGHT OF DANGER
#57 TERROR ON TRACK
#58 SPIKED!
#59 OPEN SEASON
#60 DEADFALL
#61 GRAVE DANGER
#62 FINAL GAMBIT
#63 COLD SWEAT
#64 ENDANGERED SPECIES
#65 NO MERCY
#66 THE PHOENIX EQUATION
#67 LETHAL CARGO
#68 ROUGH RIDING
#69 MAYHEM IN MOTION
#70 RIGGED FOR REVENGE

Available from ARCHWAY Paperbacks

# THE HARDY BOYS CASEFILES NO. 70

# RIGGED FOR REVENGE

## FRANKLIN W. DIXON

**AN ARCHWAY PAPERBACK**
Published by POCKET BOOKS
New York   London   Toronto   Sydney   Tokyo   Singapore

This book is a work of fiction. Names, characters, places and incidents are either the product of the author's imagination or are used fictitiously. Any resemblance to actual events or locales or persons, living or dead, is entirely coincidental.

AN ARCHWAY PAPERBACK *Original*

An Archway Paperback published by
POCKET BOOKS, a division of Simon & Schuster Inc.
1230 Avenue of the Americas, New York, NY 10020

Copyright © 1992 by Simon & Schuster Inc.
Produced by Mega-Books of New York, Inc.

ISBN: 0-671-73106-8

First Archway Paperback printing December 1992

10 9 8 7 6 5 4 3 2 1

THE HARDY BOYS, AN ARCHWAY PAPERBACK and colophon are registered trademarks of Simon & Schuster Inc.

THE HARDY BOYS CASEFILES is a trademark of Simon & Schuster Inc.

Cover art by Brian Kotzky

Printed in the U.S.A.

IL 6+

# Chapter

# 1

"HOLD THIS chopper steady!" Joe Hardy called to his brother. Frank Hardy gave a short grunt in response and quickly checked out his blond-haired younger brother. Joe sat grinning, his blue eyes twinkling, in the leather seat directly behind Frank.

"Keep your eye on the instruments, son," ordered Clem Maxwell, the tall, lean, middle-aged Texan seated next to Frank.

"Sorry." Frank returned his gaze to the glowing instrument panel of the Bell 212 helicopter he was piloting through a heavy rainstorm. This is tough enough without having Joe hassle me, Frank thought.

Frank's slim, athletic body was tense as he gripped the chopper's controls. The view out the

1

windscreen was blurred by the pelting rain. Through the raindrops and the gray, swirling shreds of cloud, Frank could just make out churning, white-capped waves a few hundred feet below.

Without warning, the chopper's controls bucked in Frank's hands. The cockpit rocked violently, buffeted by swirling winds.

"Yeee-hah!" Frank heard Joe holler. "Ride 'em, cowboy!"

Frank ignored his brother this time, concentrating instead on stabilizing the windswept craft.

"Good flying, son," Clem Maxwell said tensely. "I thought Fenton was just being a proud daddy when he claimed you could handle one of these things."

"Are you kidding?" came Joe's voice from the rear. "Frank could fly one of these babies through a hurricane."

A faint smile played beneath the Texan's bushy gray mustache. "Maybe one of these days we'll see about that," he replied.

"Thanks for the vote of confidence, Joe," Frank said modestly. "Can we talk about the case instead? Do you have any suspects yet in the sabotage, Mr. Maxwell?"

Frank and Joe's father, Fenton Hardy, an internationally famous private investigator, had been hired by the Lone Star Oil Company to check into a series of mysterious and suspicious accidents. The accidents had been plaguing Lone

Star's operations on a field of four offshore drilling rigs in the Gulf of Mexico.

Deciding he would need help on the case, Fenton had asked Frank and Joe to spend their Thanksgiving vacation undercover as oil workers on the rigs. Frank had a pilot's license, so he was given the job of flying a shuttle chopper among the four rigs. Joe would be given an office job. Together, the Hardys were to help Clem Maxwell, who was chief operating officer of the rigs, search for a saboteur.

Joe, especially, was into his role, wearing a ten-gallon cowboy hat and an ankle-length suede "duster" coat, just like the ones Texas oil men, or wildcatters, had worn in the old days. Not that Frank hadn't gotten into it a bit himself. He was sporting a leather pilot's jacket over khaki trousers and a denim shirt.

"We don't have any specific suspects, so far," Maxwell told them. "But I bet that when we find the good-for-nothing who's behind all this, he'll turn out to be a member of FOE."

"FOE?" Joe asked. "What does that stand for?"

"Federation of the Environment," Maxwell told him bitterly. "It's a radical environmental group. Their mission is good—they want to stop corporations from polluting the earth. If you ask me, though, they're just a bunch of thick-headed terrorists. Right here with Lone Star they're causing more damage to the environment than we ever could."

"How so?" Frank asked.

"Well, they started small," Maxwell said. "At first we thought it was just coincidence—a new drill bit arrived damaged, and we had to shut down Alpha rig for a day. Then someone let the oil drain out of the crane's engine on Charlie rig and the engine burned out. That shut down that rig for nearly forty-eight hours. We started to get suspicious. And they—whoever they are—stepped up their pace."

Maxwell shook his head slowly. "We were lowering an explosive charge to the ocean floor to loosen up the seabed for drilling. The explosive went off early and took out one of the concrete pylon supports on Beta rig. It's a miracle no one was hurt.

"They claim they use only peaceful means, like negotiating. But I remember what happened ten years ago, when they set off a bomb on an oil rig off the coast of Louisiana." He shook his head, scowling. "There's no way a group like that will ever change."

Frank nodded. "Dad told us about that," he said. "That bomb killed a group of workers and caused a massive oil spill, right?"

"You said it," Maxwell replied angrily. "The legal insurance costs put the oil rig operator out of business. They never even caught the guy who planted the bomb, but everybody knows FOE had to be behind it."

"Wow," Joe said quietly, hunching forward in his seat.

"From what I hear, it was horrible," the rangy Texan said thickly. "Just a mess of twisted metal, clouds of black smoke, and an ugly oil slick spreading across the Gulf of Mexico—"

Maxwell broke off, obviously disgusted. "They said you could hear the screams of the workers," he added in a low voice, "as they burned to death."

A chill ran down Frank's spine. Oil rigs—offshore rigs in particular—were among the world's most dangerous places. He wondered if he and Joe were up to finding a saboteur cold-blooded enough to kill so many.

No one said a word for a moment. All Frank heard were the howling wind and the dull, incessant beat of the chopper's rotors.

"I don't get it, though," Joe spoke up a moment later. "What makes you so sure that FOE's behind Lone Star's troubles now?"

"Because the so-called accidents we've experienced follow a pattern," said Clem, "just as they did back before the bomb."

"What kind of pattern?" Frank asked.

"We started drilling at Heron Field in the Gulf of Mexico eighteen months ago," Clem told him. "For the first year there were no problems at all. The operation seemed almost blessed. Then, in the next six months, the rigs were hit with one disaster after another. Each of the four rigs has had to shut down at least once. If we ever had to close down a rig permanently, it could cost over a million bucks."

"But aren't accidents pretty common on deep-sea drilling platforms?" Joe asked.

"They can be," Maxwell admitted. "But when they happen like clockwork, and each time to a different platform . . . Well, I don't reckon they qualify as accidents, do you?"

Frank glanced over at Maxwell. "You say the accidents happen on a regular basis," he said thoughtfully, holding the chopper steady as the wind began to pick up. "How often do the workers' shifts change on the rigs?"

"What does that have to do with it?" Joe asked.

Frank glanced back at his brother. "If all the accidents happened when a certain shift was on, that would narrow down the number of suspects," he explained.

Maxwell sounded impressed as he said, "I guess your daddy was right about your detective skills, too." He leaned back in his seat, chewing a piece of gum. "There are three shifts on this operation: White, Blue, and Red. Each shift has one hundred fifty workers," he explained. "At any given moment, there are two shifts, or about three hundred workers, on all the rigs all together. Every Monday a new shift of one hundred fifty workers comes on and one shift goes home."

"Did all the accidents happen when one particular shift was on?" Joe asked eagerly.

"You got it, Joe," Maxwell said. "And that shift is the Blue shift. I don't claim that every time the Blue shift is on we have an accident. But every time an accident has occurred, the Blue shift was on."

"I guess we're joining the Blue shift then," Frank said. "Were the people on that shift searched after Beta rig's explosion?"

"Sure," Maxwell said. "We looked for a radio transmitter that might have set off the explosive. We didn't come up with a thing. The saboteur must have tossed the radio overboard after he did his dirty work."

The Texan was rapidly chewing his gum. "Whoever's after Lone Star is playing for keeps. Deep-sea oil rigs don't come with emergency exits—"

All at once Frank's attention was switched from Maxwell to the chopper. It had begun to buck in the wind, and Frank wondered whether they were flying directly into a storm.

"What's wrong, son?" he heard Maxwell say.

"Nothing," Frank said, but he knew he sounded nervous. "I guess the storm's picking up."

Maxwell peered out at the fast-moving clouds. "You're apt to hit downdrafts in this kind of weather," he said. "If it happens, don't try to pull out of it too quickly, or you could stall."

"No need to worry," Joe called from the backseat. "As I said, Frank could fly this baby through—"

Joe was interrupted as the chopper suddenly pitched forward. Frank felt his safety belt cut into his waist. He fought the controls, but no matter what he did the chopper shook violently. It spun down toward the ocean, then pulled back.

"I can't—control it!" Frank yelled. Beads of sweat formed on his forehead as the chopper pitched and lurched again. Frank felt as though a giant hand were trying to push the small craft out of the sky.

"Do something!" Maxwell shouted. The chopper pitched forward again, and Frank instinctively pulled back on the controls. The entire cockpit shuddered violently, and Frank felt the controls go dead in his hands.

"What's happening?" Frank heard Joe shout behind him. The beat of the rotors had slowed, then stopped. The engine had stalled!

"Press the ignition!" he heard Maxwell roar. Frank pushed the button on the control panel. It was too late. The chopper began to spin in the swirling wind, and the nose slowly pitched down toward the sea. The chopper plunged like a roller coaster after the crest of a hill.

"Here we go!" Maxwell shouted, bug-eyed.

Frank stifled a scream as he saw the gray, churning, white-capped waves rise up to meet them. In another second they would crash into the water!

# Chapter

## 2

JOE STARED, fascinated, as the chopper jolted to a sudden stop and the waves disappeared from the windscreen. The chopper went dark, then filled with a dim red light.

"Bzzzz," Joe said, imitating a game show buzzer. "Thank you for playing, Frank. Please try again some other time."

"That's enough, Joe," Maxwell said with a dry chuckle. He glanced over at Frank, who was obviously shaken. "I think your brother started to believe we really were going to crash."

Joe looked at Frank, who was still staring at the computerized screen. "You forgot we were in a flight simulator?" Joe teased him. "Wow—you've got some vivid imagination."

"I reacted too quickly," Frank said with a

frown. "I should have guided the chopper out of the downdraft instead of fighting it."

"That's right," Clem Maxwell said as the simulator door automatically opened. "But you learned a valuable lesson, and you didn't get wet in the process. All our pilots use this simulator to keep up their skills. It's one of the best investments Lone Star ever made."

As the trio climbed out of the simulator, Joe saw a chubby man slightly older than Maxwell waiting for them. The man wore a business suit and a red string necktie. Joe recognized him as Dudley Baker, president of Lone Star Oil and the man who had hired their father.

"How'd he do?" Mr. Baker asked Clem Maxwell. Joe grinned to hear a Texas accent even thicker than Maxwell's.

"Not bad," Maxwell answered. "He kept it in the air almost ten minutes. Most of our trainees last less than a minute under hurricane conditions."

"I could do better if I had another chance, sir," Frank said to Mr. Baker.

"Don't worry, son." Maxwell patted Frank on the shoulder. "Hurricanes don't come around this time of year more than once or twice a century. You checked out fine."

"Good." Joe followed Frank, Maxwell, and Baker out of the simulator room. "I never knew you could get airsick without leaving the ground."

Joe removed his cowboy hat and took a seat in Mr. Baker's luxurious penthouse office. Fenton

Hardy was waiting for them in a leather wing chair facing the president's desk. Joe gazed through the plate-glass wall at a panoramic, sun-drenched view of downtown Houston.

"I still feel like I'm flying," he said as the others took their seats.

"Some view, isn't it?" Baker said from behind his desk. "Now, let's get down to business." He nodded at Clem to continue.

Clem Maxwell sat up straighter. "The boys will leave with the next shift for Heron Field at noon today. There's a vacant spot for a chopper pilot for Frank."

"What about me?" Joe asked, balancing his hat on his knees.

"You've been assigned as administrative assistant to T. H. Hunnicut," Maxwell told him. "She's chief operating officer for HomeBase."

"I thought that was *your* job," Joe said.

"I run the oil rigs," Maxwell explained. "But on HomeBase, Hunnicut is the boss. HomeBase is our flotel, a floating hotel where the workers live and eat."

"Administrative assistant," Joe mused with a glance at his brother. "That sounds important."

Mr. Baker chuckled. "You'll be the most important gofer on HomeBase," he assured Joe.

"You mean while I'm soaring through the sky in my own chopper, Joe's going to be a glorified errand boy?" Frank sat back and grinned.

Maxwell snorted. "Don't get a big head," he said to Frank. "You won't be much more than a glorified taxi driver, ferrying men and supplies back and forth from HomeBase to each of the four drilling rigs. And you won't be piloting a Chinook, either. You'll be in one of them itty-bitty Bell helicopters.''

Now it was Joe's turn to grin.

"What will you be doing while we're on the rigs, Dad?" Frank asked their father.

"I'll start by running background checks on all the Blue shift workers," Fenton Hardy replied. He held up a creased sheet of paper for his sons to see. "I'll also try to track down the source of this note. Mr. Baker received this less than an hour ago. It's a threat against Lone Star Oil—so at least we know the sabotage hasn't been a product of anyone's overworked imagination.''

"Wow! Let me see." Joe took the note from his father's hand, and Frank leaned in to read it over Joe's shoulder. " 'Stop drilling off shore now,' " Joe read out loud. " 'Or else Lone Star will be destroyed.' "

"These letters were ripped out of magazines," he said. "How are you going to figure out where it came from?" Joe asked his father.

"It won't be easy," Fenton admitted, "but I'm starting to think Mr. Maxwell is right. This may be the work of a terrorist organization like FOE.''

"We do have other suspects," Mr. Baker told the boys. "Heron Oil Field is in Mexican waters. The oil belongs to PetroMex, a company owned by the Mexican government. They hired us, Lone Star, to pump the oil because we're the only company with the right equipment to drill for oil in water that deep.''

Frank asked, "What does that have to do with sabotage?"

"Everything, I'm afraid," Mr. Baker said. "This is a very sensitive business deal. We're the first American company to work a Mexican oil field, and it was not a popular decision in Mexico to hire us. As part of the deal, I agreed that half of the workers would be Mexican citizens.''

"And you suspect a Mexican worker is sabotaging the rigs?'' Joe asked.

"It's possible," Baker said. "From what Clem tells me, some of the Mexicans resent working for Americans.''

"Sabotage is a pretty extreme way to protest,'' Frank pointed out. "Besides, if they caused an environmental disaster, they'd be destroying their own land.''

"Your dad had the idea that the saboteur could be an American worker trying to set up the Mexicans,'' Baker continued.

"No way," Clem Maxwell said, shaking his head. "All my men—Americans and Mexicans—are hard workers. I'm telling you, FOE is responsible. I feel it in my gut.''

"Mr. Maxwell told us it would cost a million dollars if you had to shut down a rig," Joe said.

The company president became haggard looking. "He's right. A shutdown would be a catastrophe. But these accidents have already cost so much that if you don't find the troublemaker by the end of the week, I'll have to shut down the entire field."

Mr. Baker swiveled his chair around to gaze out the window. "Lone Star is my life," he said somberly. "And if Heron Field goes, Lone Star goes, too."

"Mr. Baker really knows how to put pressure on a guy," Joe remarked half an hour later as the three Hardys rode in a taxi to the Lone Star heliport. "If we don't figure out who's destroying Heron Field, his lifework goes down the tubes."

"It's a tough case," Fenton Hardy agreed. "With one hundred fifty people in Blue shift alone, it'll be a major job just to narrow down the list of suspects."

"What scares me most is that Heron Field sounds like a major environmental disaster waiting to happen," Frank pointed out. "I don't understand why an environmental group like FOE would try to pollute the Gulf as a protest against tampering with the environment. It doesn't make sense."

"That's why we're checking all the angles," Fenton reminded him. "Joe, you're responsible for checking in with me every day you're out there. Use the radio in your office on HomeBase when no one's around. You can leave messages for me through the Lone Star office."

As the cab turned off the main road and headed down a service road toward the Lone Star heliport, Joe gazed out the window. The airport was small, just a terminal building, a large hangar, and a small control tower, all surrounded by a ten-foot-high chain-link fence.

"Look," Joe said, "the helicopter's already waiting."

He pointed to a large Chinook helicopter outside the terminal. It was about the size of a city bus and had two rotors: one over the cockpit, the other near the tail. The chopper was white, with the Lone Star logo painted in bright red.

"Be careful out there," Fenton Hardy said as the taxi pulled up to the side of the road opposite the terminal.

Joe gave his father a wide grin. "Come on, Dad. How dangerous can an office job be?"

"If I know you, you'll be out on the rigs the first chance you get," Fenton replied as the boys unloaded their duffel bags. "Just remember—a floating rig is no place to get careless."

"Message received." Frank gave their father a mock salute. As the taxi pulled away, Fenton returned it with a farewell nod.

"Okay," Joe heard his brother say, "we're strangers who just happened to catch the same cab from town."

"Excuse me?" Joe adjusted his cowboy hat. "Do I know you, pardner?"

"Just keep that dumb duster out of my face." Frank laughed, pushing at the material as it flapped in the breeze. "And you can call me sir."

Joe chuckled as he stepped off the curb to cross the road to the terminal.

"Joe!" Frank yelled, reaching for his brother's arm.

Joe glanced back over his shoulder. At the same moment he heard an enormous roar. A huge black Harley-Davidson motorcycle was speeding toward the brothers from around the corner of the terminal.

"Jump!" Frank tugged on his brother's arm.

Joe was too startled to move and could only stare in horror as the motorcycle roared straight toward them!

## Chapter

# 3

"AAAGH!" With a renewed burst of strength, Frank yanked Joe backward to the curb an instant before the huge motorcycle roared past. They fell onto the ground and stared at the black bike as it skidded to a stop thirty feet away.

A very tall, sinewy man flipped down the kickstand with a massive black cowboy boot. He turned around and stared at the Hardys. "Watch where you're going, boys!" he shouted. "I nearly creamed you!"

"You watch where *you're* going," Frank shot back. "This isn't the Indianapolis Speedway."

The driver dismounted and jogged back toward the Hardys. Frank eyed him warily as he helped Joe to his feet. The man's plain T-shirt revealed hard, oversize muscles, and his face was tanned dark above his beard. He was probably only in

17

his late twenties, but the sun had already etched deep lines around his eyes and forehead.

"You're right," the driver admitted. "I did take that corner too fast. You get tempted sometimes, on a bike like mine. No hard feelings, I hope." He stared curiously from Frank to Joe. "Are you guys flying to Heron Field?"

"Yeah, on the noon flight," Joe said. "In fact, we're running late."

The driver extended his hand to both boys. "I'm Dave Rubel. I do equipment maintenance on the rigs."

"Joe Laurel," Joe said, using the alias he and Frank had agreed on beforehand. To Frank's amusement Joe winced visibly at Rubel's grip.

"This your first time out?" Rubel asked, letting go of Joe's hand and peering intently at him. "Don't think I've seen you around before."

"I'm new," Joe replied warily. "I was hired as an administrative assistant. And this is Frank Lee."

"I'm a newcomer, too," Frank told Rubel. "I'll be a chopper pilot, transporting equipment."

"Well, welcome to the most boring time of your lives, guys," Rubel said with a wry expression. "In about a week you're going to want to be back on dry land so bad you won't be able to see straight."

"It's that bad?" Joe asked.

"What—two weeks crammed onto a rig the size of a postage stamp?" Rubel answered. "Then there are the red alerts that go off on this project practically every day. One minute you're on the job, the next you're ducking for cover. And nothing around to save you but the deep blue sea."

"Wow," Joe said, frowning. "I hadn't thought about that. You've worked at Heron since the beginning of the project?"

"From the first day," the biker told him. "It's the worst rig I've ever worked on, by far." He gave a dry laugh. "Well, don't take my word for it. You'll find out soon enough." With a wave, he started off toward his motorcycle. "See you in the chopper," he added.

"That's one weird guy," Joe remarked in a low voice as the two watched Rubel roar off toward the airfield. "Did you see the way he kept staring at us? You don't think he saw through our cover, do you?"

"No way." Frank hoisted his duffel bag back onto his shoulder. "We didn't do anything to give ourselves away. He was probably just trying to be friendly."

"Great," Joe said as they started toward the airfield on foot. "The most boring time of our lives."

Not bad, Joe said to himself, stowing his duffel bag in the overhead compartment of the Chinook helicopter. This is almost like a commercial jetliner.

Joe glanced around the cabin, which seated about forty. Frank occupied a seat near the front. Dave Rubel entered the cabin, stooping to avoid hitting his head, and sat down beside Frank. Joe removed his duster, folded it carefully, and buckled himself into his window seat just as someone sat down beside him.

"Howdy," Joe said, trying out a Texas greeting on the pale young man next to him. "Joe Laurel, administrative assistant." He stuck out his hand. "Who are you?"

"Matt Blaine." The young man spoke without a trace of a Texan accent. With his wide blue eyes and round glasses, Blaine appeared to be almost as young as Joe. "Pleased to meet you, Joe. This your first trip offshore?"

"How did you know?" Joe asked, disgruntled.

"I can always spot a rookie," Blaine said with a laugh. "Don't worry about it. Offshore work's a breeze. You do your shift, and then you get a nice long break to spend some of that fat paycheck they give you. I've been working the rigs for two years now. I'm saving up to retire by the time I'm thirty-five."

Joe glanced out the window and saw Clem Maxwell trot across the field toward the Chinook. He was followed by two pilots, sharing a joke and slapping each other on the back.

A few moments later a pilot's voice boomed over the intercom. "Howdy, boys. We'll be taking off in about two minutes," the voice said. "The weather's clear out over the Gulf, so we should have y'all at Heron Field in about six hours. *Hasta luego.*"

Further conversation was impossible as the

sound of the beating rotors and droning engines filled the chopper. The noise beat against Joe's ears, and the chopper vibrated violently. Then, suddenly, Joe felt the chopper lift into the air, like a balloon suddenly freed from its string.

Once they were airborne, the noise of the engines lessened. Joe turned to his companion.

"Someone else told me that offshore work is incredibly boring," he said. "You're cooped up on a rig with nothing to do."

Blaine laughed. "You think that's bad?" he said with a grin. "I'm going in-sat. But it's great—like nothing else on this planet."

"In-sat?" Joe asked. "What's that?"

"You really are a rookie, aren't you?" Blaine joked. "In-sat means in-saturation. I'm a diver. I repair the pipelines that take the oil from the wells back to shore. That means I spend my workdays five hundred feet under the water."

Joe whistled. "I've done a little diving myself, but nothing like that."

"And I bet you've never been on a dive that lasted four weeks," Blaine said.

"Four weeks?" Joe couldn't understand how anyone could stay underwater that long.

"It's like this," Blaine explained. "Deep Six is a floating, movable platform. We divers stay in a pressurized chamber that is on board Deep Six. It's called being in-sat because the atmosphere in the chamber is saturated with helium and oxygen, and has the same high pressure as

21

water at a depth of five hundred feet. Are you following me?" he asked Joe.

"I think so," Joe said. "So while you're on assignment you stay inside the chamber."

"Right," Blaine said. "Our chamber on Deep Six is home while we're in-sat—it has beds, bathrooms—we even get fed in it. Deep Six takes us to the spots on the pipeline that need repairs. Our chamber is connected to a diving bell, which is also pressurized. Every day we crawl into the bell and go down to work on the ocean floor."

"What happens when your shift is up?" Joe asked.

"After our three and a half weeks on the job, we spend four days decompressing. Then they spring us from the tank and we go home for a couple of weeks."

"I've heard of on-the-job pressure before," Joe said, "but that's ridiculous."

Blaine groaned. "Do me a favor, rook," he said. "Don't become a diver. I'd hate to spend four weeks in-sat with jokes like that!"

Frank watched the shadow of the Chinook skim the white-capped ocean waves a thousand feet below. Dave Rubel snored loudly in the seat next to him. Rubel had fallen asleep almost as soon as he had sat down. Frank glanced at him and wondered what the chances were that Rubel was their saboteur. Surely, Frank thought, the culprit wouldn't be at ease enough to fall asleep.

Frank glanced at his watch. It was almost six

o'clock, and the sun was beginning to lower toward the western horizon.

"Attention, folks." The pilot's voice crackled over the intercom. "We're approaching Heron Field. We'll be letting you down on Home Base in about ten minutes, so sit down and buckle up."

Frank peered out the window. In the distance, framed against the blue sky, he saw the group of oil rigs. They jutted up out of the waves like a collection of Eiffel Towers dropped into the middle of the ocean.

As they approached the oil field, Frank gasped at the size of the rigs. Each platform was roughly as large as a football field, sitting on four huge concrete pylons. Frank noted that the largest platform stood six stories high above its pylons. It was a three-dimensional maze of girders, rails, and steel beams.

As they flew closer, Frank noted that each of the large platforms had two immense towers rising hundreds of feet above it. He remembered reading that the towers were called derricks. He knew that one derrick on each platform housed the huge drill used to dig new wells five hundred feet below the surface of the ocean. Each platform's second derrick was topped with a billowing yellow flame. The excess natural gas piped up from the wells was burned to prevent explosions down in the wells.

The Chinook helicopter began to circle to the left of the rigs, providing Frank with a close-up view of each one. In the distance, Frank saw their immediate destination, a platform as broad as the others but without any derricks. It sat lower in the water, too, Frank saw, probably only four stories above the ocean. The platform was perched on two huge submarines, making it mobile. That was their home base.

As they passed the last oil derricks, Rubel stirred and yawned. "Quite a sight, isn't it?" he said.

Frank nodded and continued to stare out the window.

When the Chinook finally arrived at Home Base, Frank could see a large octagonal landing pad. Painted on the landing pad was a large yellow circle with a huge white *H* centered in it. That's a sight I'll have to get used to, Frank thought as the chopper hung over the landing pad. From that height, the landing pad was distressingly small.

Suddenly the helicopter dropped straight down toward the middle of the circle. Frank's stomach rose to his throat. He felt a gentle thud and heard the helicopter's engines cut off. They were at Heron Field.

"Well, here goes nothing," Rubel remarked as the passengers began unbuckling their seat belts and gathering their belongings. Frank saw Joe take his duffel bag from the overhead bin. Their eyes met, and Joe nodded toward the door. Frank understood the message: they should wait and leave the helicopter together after the others had gone.

While Joe put on his duster, grabbed his duffel bag, and started down the aisle, Frank glanced one more time out the window. The other workers had already crossed the landing pad and were descending a steel staircase. A stiff breeze blew, and several workers had to hang onto their cowboy hats and baseball caps.

"Fun. Yeah." Frank tried not to think of setting a chopper down on that tiny landing pad. "At least it's sunny. Hard to believe it's the end of November."

When Frank and Joe stepped out of the chopper, Frank felt a chill in the salty ocean breeze. "Whoa!" he heard Joe say, grabbing his cowboy hat to keep it from flying away. His long duster flapped around him. "I didn't know it would be so windy."

Just as Frank started down the steps, an ear-splitting siren went off. Ahead of him, the other workers were quickly crowding down the steel staircase off the launching pad.

"Red alert!" bellowed a voice from an unseen loudspeaker. "This is not a drill! Isolate all ignition sources! Choppers, evacuate helipads! All hands report immediately to duty hazard positions! Repeat, this is not a drill!"

Frank stumbled down the steps of the helicopter, with Joe close behind. At their backs, one of the pilots slammed the hatch shut. Frank and Joe ducked as the Chinook's rotors fired up, beating the air over their heads. "Hey!" Frank heard Joe yell. "What's that?"

"What's what?" Frank turned toward his brother as the huge chopper began to lift off. Frank's heart skipped a beat when he saw what was wrong. The end of Joe's duster had been caught in the helicopter's door!

"Joe!" Frank screamed as Joe yanked on his duster, trying to pull himself loose. It was too late. As Joe kicked his feet wildly, the Chinook rose from the pad, dragging its helpless passenger into the air.

# Chapter

## 4

"GRAB MY LEGS, Frank!" Joe yelled as the chopper lifted him off the landing pad, his duster spread capelike above his head. He struggled to get out of the sleeves, but his arms were hopelessly tangled.

"I've got them!" Frank yelled from below.

Joe felt his brother's hands tugging on his ankles as he drifted toward the edge of the platform. Joe stared over the edge at the waves crashing four stories below. With a last desperate effort, Joe twisted his body to escape from his duster.

Joe heard a ripping sound as the sleeves separated from his duster. Before he could warn Frank, Joe plunged to the surface of the platform, directly onto his brother.

"Oof!" Frank gasped, breaking his brother's

fall. Joe rolled off him right away, but Frank remained motionless. The siren was still wailing, and the chopper had soared into the sky.

"Frank, are you okay?" Joe demanded.

Frank opened his eyes, then sat up slowly and rubbed his shoulder. "Am *I* okay?" he answered unsteadily. "What about *you?*"

"The duster's gone and my hat blew overboard, but I'm fine," Joe said, helping Frank to his feet. He removed the ripped sleeves and jammed them into his duffel bag. "Let's get out of here."

"Hold on just a minute!" Joe heard someone yell over the noise of the siren. He turned to see a pencil-thin man standing at the edge of the helipad. The man's long, stringy hair was blowing straight up from his balding head. He sported a narrow mustache and clutched a clipboard in one hand. "You must be the new guys."

"That's right," said Frank as the boys joined him. "I'm Frank Lee, and this is Joe Laurel."

"I'm Darryl Purdy," the tall man said, "assistant operating officer on Home Base. You boys need to get below. There's been another accident on Alpha rig."

"What happened?" Frank asked as he and Joe followed Purdy toward the steps.

"The chain on the hoist broke," Purdy said, leading the way downstairs. "The hoist lifts pieces of oil pipe up to where we can connect them to the drill pipe. It has a chain that acts like a pulley. When the chain broke, the hoist

28

collapsed and dropped thirty feet. Didn't you guys see it?"

"No." Joe clattered down the steps behind him. "I guess it happened right when we were leaving the chopper. Was anyone hurt?"

"Two guys were hit by falling debris. One is in critical condition. They're already being air-lifted out. No idea why it happened yet. That chain was brand-new, just shipped out a week ago."

As they reached the bottom of the steps, the siren stopped. Joe heard the static of a nearby loudspeaker.

"Attention," blared the voice. "Condition red has been terminated. Condition green prevails. Resume all normal activities."

"Why'd they order everyone to run for cover here on Home Base if the accident happened on Alpha rig?" Joe asked, jogging down a narrow passageway behind the quick-moving Purdy. A row of large tanks lined one side of the passageway. On the other side was a corrugated-metal wall.

"It's a safety precaution," Purdy said over his shoulder. "If something happens on any of the other platforms, we go on red alert. That just means we have to turn off all our machinery, get below, and stand by to help out if necessary. Blue alert's what you have to watch out for. That's when something's happened here on Home Base."

He whipped around a corner, and Joe and

Frank hurried after him. "Thelma Hunnicut has the alerting system down to a science," he said dryly. "Well, here we are." He led them through a door in the metal wall. "The Admin office. My home and now yours, Joe."

"Admin?" Joe asked.

Purdy gave him a funny look. "Short for *administration*. I thought you had some office experience."

"I'm just shaken up from the alert, that's all. So this is where I get to work."

His face fell as he surveyed the room. It was like a small, cramped doctor's office, with fluorescent lights, steel walls without windows, and a rubber mat covering the floor instead of carpet. A counter divided the room in half. The near half of the room held nothing but a few folding chairs. The far half held two desks stacked with papers, and rows of filing cabinets. A door in the opposite wall led to an inner office. It didn't look like a center of activity to Joe.

"This is it," Purdy said proudly. "And am I glad you finally showed up. Thelma's been without an assistant for three days now. She's driving me nuts."

"Come on," Joe said, chuckling. "She can't be that bad."

"Purdy!" bellowed a voice from the inner office. At the sound of it, Joe saw Purdy flinch like a scolded puppy. "Is that my new gofer?"

Joe saw a woman appear in the doorway of the inner office. His jaw dropped open. The woman was around forty years old, with flame red hair framing a fashion model's face. She was as tall as Joe, and wore dark pants and an olive-drab shirt and tie over a slim but curvaceous figure. Crossing her arms, she checked Joe out.

"This is him, Thelma," Purdy said timidly. "Joe Laurel, meet your new boss, Thelma Hunnicut."

Joe took a deep breath and stepped forward to shake his boss's hand. "Pleased to meet you, ma'am."

Ms. Hunnicut shook his hand with a skeptical expression. "What day-care center did this one come from?" she said to Purdy.

Joe blushed. "I didn't hire him," he heard Purdy defend himself. "Maxwell brought him in. The word came right from the top."

"I get it," Hunnicut said, her eyes still fixed on Joe. "Friends in high places, huh? The little pup wants to experience life on the rigs before heading off to college?"

"I came here to work," Joe said resentfully.

"Good." Hunnicut smiled coolly. "We'll try to accommodate you." She turned to Purdy. "Show Blondie and his friend to their evac stations."

"Blondie?" Frank laughed before he could stop himself.

"After he eats, make sure he comes straight back to my office." She looked at Joe. "You have tons of paperwork to process, Blondie." She tossed him a key she'd been holding in one hand. "I'll leave instructions on my desk. When

I get here in the morning I expect those instructions to have been followed to the letter—or else.''

"Yes, ma'am," Joe said, just barely controlling his temper.

"Good. Your job is to do what you're told and keep your mouth shut the rest of the time." Frowning, she turned back to Purdy and snapped, "I have work to do. Get them out of here."

"Right, Thelma," Purdy said. He started out the door, followed by Frank and his stunned and unhappy younger brother.

"Blondie!" Joe muttered to himself as they headed back down the passageway. "Some way to spend a vacation!"

Frank grinned as he followed Purdy, knowing what Joe was thinking. What I wouldn't give to be a fly on the wall when those two work together, he thought. If Joe can hold his temper with Thelma Hunnicut, he's a lot cooler than I thought.

Purdy led the boys down another, shorter set of stairs and onto an exterior catwalk that ran along the outside of the platform. Frank inhaled deeply, relieved to be outside. Home Base had felt like a prison with its steel walls and rubber carpets. The catwalk was precarious, but at least they could enjoy the view of the Gulf.

"You two are assigned to the same evacuation station," Purdy said, checking his clipboard as he led them to the end of the catwalk. He seemed to have regained his confidence now that he was out of Hunnicut's range. "Next time a red alert sounds, this is where you come."

"You're sure there'll be a next time?" Frank asked.

"Are you kidding?" Purdy stopped at the end of the catwalk, took a large handkerchief from his back pocket, and mopped his forehead. Then he lowered his voice. "Those accidents aren't going to stop until these rigs are closed down. The whole place is plain jinxed. If it was up to me, I'd shut the whole field down before anyone else gets hurt."

Frank and Joe stared at him, astonished. Did Purdy really believe Heron Field was jinxed, Frank wondered? Or could he be trying to spread rumors to force Mr. Baker to shut down the rigs? Could this thin, nervous man be a FOE member? The idea made Frank grin.

"There's nothing funny about it," Purdy snapped. He turned his back on Frank and placed a hand on top of a large fiberglass lifeboat that dangled from chains off the side of the platform. The boat was large enough for twenty people and covered with a canvas tarp. "Next alert, drop everything and come here. This baby is your ticket to safety."

Frank realized that Purdy was peering off into the western sky. Following his gaze, Frank spotted another Chinook moving toward them.

"Here come our Mexican friends." Purdy's nasty tone surprised Frank. Abruptly, the office worker turned and started back down the cat-walk the way they'd come. "Lee, after dinner you report to the flight control office at helipad A," he said. "The nightly pilots' debriefing is at eight-thirty. Alvarez—your boss—likes to meet his pilots the day they arrive."

"Check," Frank said.

"As for you," Purdy said to Joe as he showed them to the stairwell leading to their cabins, "keep Thelma happy. Got it? I need to keep that woman off my back."

Half an hour later Frank entered the large, well-lit employee cafeteria on level A. The cafeteria was one flight above the workers' cabins, which to Frank's surprise had been neat and attractive. Though the rooms were small, each was furnished with a set of bunk beds, two desks, two dressers, and a bathroom shared with the cabin next door. Clearly an effort had been made to ensure the workers' comfort, though the steel walls and no windows made the space claustrophobic.

The effect was even worse here in the cafeteria, Frank realized. With so many men crowded into one space, the tension was overwhelming.

Frank scanned the men standing in the food line, then those at the dozens of round tables scattered throughout the room. He was looking for Joe. He noticed that the American workers were sitting on one side of the room, while the Mexican contingent sat on the other. No one spoke above a quiet murmur. It was almost as though everyone was holding his breath, waiting for something to happen.

I doubt this is the atmosphere Lone Star and PetroMex had in mind, Frank reflected. His eyes wandered to the line of empty tables that divided the two groups. They were empty except for the table nearest the serving line, where Joe Hardy sat gobbling down a huge steak. Frank chuckled and walked up to his table.

"This food is unreal," Joe said, swallowing. "Like Sunday dinner, and all you can eat."

"Glad you like it," said a voice at Frank's elbow. He turned to see Dave Rubel standing beside him. "It's one of the things they do to help us pass the time. We get no newspapers, no cable TV. Just a weight room downstairs—for those who don't get enough exercise out on the rig—and a few videotapes we've all memorized." The biker pulled out a chair. "Mind if I join you?"

"Go right ahead," Joe said. "You can tell me about all the other menus."

"I'm going to get some grub," Frank said. He left to join the line.

As he waited, Frank eyed the clusters of Mexican workers. They seemed quiet, though a few of them returned the Americans' hostile glances. Frank wondered when the trouble between the groups had started.

His thoughts were interrupted just then by the sound of hearty laughter. It seemed out of place in such a gloomy atmosphere. Frank turned to see a tall, handsome Mexican man throwing his head back and enjoying a belly laugh. The man sat at a crowded table, like a king holding court. The others at his table chuckled, too. There's one guy who's not afraid to break the ice, Frank thought. He wondered who the man was, and what—or whom—he was laughing at.

Frank returned to Joe's table to find that Darryl Purdy had joined Joe and Dave Rubel. The thin, balding office worker was watching Rubel shovel in food.

"The atmosphere's kind of uptight in here, don't you think?" Frank heard Joe asking Purdy. "I mean—the two groups divided up this way. What's going on?"

"You got me," Purdy said with a cough. "It's been like this from the beginning."

"Come on, Purdy, you know what the problem is," Rubel said, impatiently cutting into his steak. "The Mexicans think we Americans are horning in on territory that doesn't belong to us."

"Right, and a lot of Americans are saying the Mexicans had better straighten out their attitudes," Purdy retorted angrily. "Without us, they wouldn't be getting this oil."

"You think one of the Mexicans might have caused today's accident on the rig?" Frank asked casually.

Both men glared at Frank. "How should we

know?" Rubel muttered. "I just do my job and keep my head down."

"That's the way it should be." Frank was surprised to see the glint in Purdy's eye as he glared at Rubel. "Because as you know, Rubel, no one on this field is irreplaceable."

Just then, someone brushed past their table, accidentally elbowing Purdy. Purdy jerked back, causing the man behind him to spill an entire cup of coffee down Purdy's back.

"Hey!" Purdy cried, wheeling around. The man who had bumped him was a short, nervous-looking Mexican worker. "Watch where you're going, *amigo!*"

The room fell silent as everyone watched the confrontation

*"Lo siento,"* the Mexican said to Purdy. Frank knew that the man was apologizing.

"Speak English, *amigo,*" Purdy snapped. "This is an American operation!"

"Come on, Darryl, chill out," Joe said, rising.

"Keep out of this, kid," Purdy growled. Then he turned toward the tables of Mexican workers, who were watching the scene with expressions of dread.

"I've had about enough of their attitude," Purdy yelled in their direction. "It's bad enough that they think we're stealing jobs from them, when their government forced us to hire them— even though they can't cut the work."

A hush fell over the room. Frank watched as the Mexican worker's face turned red with rage.

Before Frank could move, the man had swung a roundhouse blow to Purdy's jaw, sending the thin man sprawling into Frank's dinner.

Instantly the room erupted. A group of American workers rushed toward the Mexican who had attacked Purdy. Behind them, Mexicans and Americans rushed at one another.

"Hey! Everyone settle down!" Frank heard Joe yell as he stepped between two fighting groups. Instantly he disappeared into a mass of brawling men.

"Joe!" Frank bellowed, stepping onto their table. Fights were breaking out all around the cafeteria. Frank had to duck to avoid flying plates and chairs. From atop the table, Frank saw Purdy, who had started the fight, slink out the door. Then he spotted Joe in the heart of the riot, swinging wildly at both sides, attempting to break free.

"Joe!" Frank leapt into the middle of the crowd, determined to help his brother. He lashed out at the fists and elbows that pummeled him. Then he lost his balance and slid across the floor, tumbling hard into some trash cans. In a flash two Mexicans leapt on him, pinning him down by the shoulders, yelling at each other in Spanish.

"I didn't do anything!" Frank shouted as one of the Mexican workers grabbed a steak knife from the floor beside him.

"Your friend started this," one of his captors shouted back with a heavy accent. "He's been after us since we got here. We've had enough insults from you *Americanos!*"

Why me? Frank wondered, struggling against his captors. He'd only just arrived, and they were going to make an example of him already!

Frank felt the cold steel of the knife blade as it was pressed against his throat. Are they going to kill me? he wondered dimly. From what seemed like far away, he heard his brother call his name.

# Chapter

## 5

"FRANK!" Joe pushed through the fighting workers to his brother. The sound of Joe's voice caused the man holding the knife to turn around. In one fluid motion, Joe grabbed a plate and flung it Frisbee-style at the man. The plate struck him on the side of the head, stunning him.

That was close, Joe thought as Frank used his newly freed hand to punch his other assailant in the jaw. Knocking the man to one side, Frank leapt to his feet.

The fray was interrupted by a bellowed *"Basta!"* Joe spun around to find the source of the sound. The speaker stood in the center of the room with his hands on his hips. Joe heard his brother say, "I saw that man joking around with the other Mexicans earlier."

"Enough!" another voice roared from the far

side of the room in the meantime. Joe turned and saw Clem Maxwell standing in the doorway, gazing angrily at the wrecked cafeteria.

The tall, handsome Mexican worker shouted an order in Spanish to his friends. They moved back to their side of the room. Joe noted that many of them now sported cuts or bruises.

"You clowns had better stop this nonsense, and now," Maxwell snapped in his Texas drawl to the American workers as they, too, returned to their tables. "Here we have a man in critical condition in a Houston hospital, and you morons are hurting each other on purpose?"

Maxwell shook his head in disgust, his eyes narrowed, surveying the room. His gaze passed over Joe and Frank without seeming to recognize them. "Sharpe! Thompson! Rubel!" he snapped. "Y'all are on cleanup detail. I want this mess gone in an hour. No buts!" he added when the three men opened their mouths to protest.

Joe watched the tall Mexican worker respond by ordering three of his group to help in the cleanup, too. Maxwell crossed the room and shook the tall man by the hand.

*"Lo siento,* Lopez," he said gruffly.

"I'm sorry, too," Lopez replied in perfect English. "Let's hope it doesn't happen again."

"You don't have any idea how this started, do you?"

Lopez's eyes burned as he glanced over at the

Hardys' table. Like the rest of the workers, Frank held his breath.

"No, I don't," Lopez said at last, his eyes sliding away from the Hardys and back to Maxwell. "But whoever it is, I'm sure he regrets this as much as we do."

As Frank and Joe headed for the door, Frank muttered in his brother's ear, "Why do you think Lopez let Purdy off the hook like that?"

"Who knows?" Joe said with a shrug. "The guy sure didn't deserve it. Did you see how he started the fight and then sneaked off so he wouldn't get hurt?"

"There's something weird about him," Frank agreed thoughtfully. "If he hates the idea of a cooperative venture with Mexico, why'd he sign up for this job?" Frank glanced at his brother. "I'm beginning to think Mr. Baker's theory makes a lot of sense."

"That a group of Mexicans are sabotaging the place?" Joe asked as they entered the stairwell and climbed a flight of stairs. Most of the other diners had gone downstairs, probably to the weight room or video room, and the Hardys were out of earshot.

"Maybe," Frank said. "But keep your ears open. I'm due at my pilots' meeting. I'll see if I can get them to talk about the accidents. And while you're working tonight in Hunnicut's office, maybe you can sneak in a call to Dad on the shortwave radio. He probably heard about the accident, so we should let him know we're okay."

"I'll also ask him to check out Purdy's background," Joe agreed. "And Lopez's, if he can. If any Mexican is plotting sabotage, Lopez'd probably know about it."

They exited the staircase and headed down one of the narrow corridors just belowdecks. "I'll see if I can get a look at the personnel files, too." Joe lowered his voice as they passed a pair of workers on their way to the infirmary. When the Hardys were again out of earshot, he added, "By the way, do you think Dave Rubel's onto us? He sure has been hanging around us a lot."

Frank shrugged. "Check out his personnel file," he suggested. "Check whether anyone was on that rig that FOE blew up ten years ago. That might give us a real lead."

They had reached the small ladder leading up to the surface of the platform. "Let's meet by our evac station at ten o'clock," Frank said to his brother. "No one will see us there. We can talk about what to do next."

Joe gave a mock salute. "Wish me luck with my Amazon boss."

"Good luck—" Frank didn't have the heart to call Joe "Blondie" again. He chuckled to himself and started up the ladder.

It was pitch-black outside when Frank stepped onto the platform. The only sounds were the howling wind and the distant roar of the oil rigs. On the far side of the helipad, Frank spotted a large building with walls of corrugated metal. A huge open doorway two stories high revealed a cavernous interior, brightly lit. That must be the hangar where the choppers are housed, Frank realized.

He lowered his head and made his way toward the hangar, entering through a normal-size door to the right of the larger entrance. Inside, he found a small room crammed full of filing cabinets, radio equipment, and a large chalkboard with a roster of the day's flights written on it. Frank noticed a scrawled entry in the afternoon slot, written in different-colored chalk. "Emergency transport, City Hospital, Houston," the notation read. "Alpha rig, chopper D."

Frank turned from the blackboard to a man sitting in front of the radio set in the corner of the dimly lit room. The man wore a headset and was speaking into a microphone, his face lit an eerie green by the radar screen nearby. The man noticed Frank and turned to face him.

"Howdy. What's up?" he said, keeping his headphones on.

"The name's Lee," Frank said. "I'm a new pilot. I'm here to meet Alvarez."

"They're all in the weather booth." The man nodded toward a short flight of stairs in the opposite corner of the room. "Something's up. You'd better get there."

As he ran upstairs, Frank heard a distinctive voice rise.

"Get real," Thelma Hunnicut shouted from within the weather booth. "It's a question of safety!" The rest of her words were drowned out in a chorus of other voices raised in argument.

Frank reached the top of the stairs to find a room very much like the one below, complete with more filing cabinets, another radio set, and even more electronic equipment along one wall. Sitting in the center of the room, in the midst of a heated discussion, were Thelma Hunnicut, Clem Maxwell, and half a dozen men Frank didn't recognize.

When they saw Frank, the arguers fell silent. A middle-aged man with dark skin and black, curly hair frowned at the interruption. "Who are you?" he asked curtly.

"I'm a new pilot," Frank said, stepping forward uneasily. "Frank Lee."

"Ah! Yes." The dark-haired man eyed Frank appraisingly. "I'm Alvarez, your coordinator." He hesitated. "You're a bit young for this assignment, aren't you?"

"They're all kids these days," Hunnicut said glumly. "You should see the cherub I got saddled with."

"I did okay on the flight simulator," Frank said defensively. He turned to Maxwell. "Right, sir?"

"Second highest score ever," the Texan told the others. The other men in the room, who were younger and whom Frank guessed were pilots, shifted uncomfortably.

Alvarez seemed pleased. "Good," he said, smiling at Frank and revealing a set of extraordinarily white teeth. "We're going to need good pilots this week."

"Uh—if you don't mind my asking, sir," Frank said, "why?"

Alvarez stopped smiling. "This is our meteorologist, Todd Jenkins." He nodded to the rotund young man who sat beside him. "He just gave us some very bad news. Tell him, Jenkins."

The meteorologist cleared his throat. "There's a storm developing off Cuba," he told Frank as though he had already given the news several times. "It's a bit early to tell for sure how it will develop. But the way it looks now, it could be a big one."

"A big one?" Frank repeated.

"You dolt," Hunnicut snapped. "He's talking about a hurricane. It's picking up power over the ocean, and it's heading straight for Heron Field!"

# Chapter

## 6

A SILENCE fell over the group huddled in the crowded room.

"This is not to be repeated to anyone," Clem Maxwell warned Frank sternly. "We don't want to cause panic among the men."

"I won't tell anyone, sir," Frank assured him. "But doesn't this mean we should evacuate the rigs? A fleet of Chinooks from the mainland could get everyone safely ashore within ten hours."

"That's what I say," chimed in Hunnicut. "Let's not take any more stupid chances."

Any more chances? Frank wondered. What other chances with the men's lives had they already taken?

His thoughts were interrupted by Maxwell's voice asking Jenkins how long it would be before the storm arrived.

"About twenty-four hours," Jenkins replied, "assuming that it comes this way." He gave Hunnicut a pointed look. "It could easily veer off at any moment."

"How long until you can determine its true severity?" Maxwell snapped, all business now.

"We'll have a handle on it within eight hours—ten at the most," Jenkins told him.

"There, you see?" Maxwell said to Hunnicut, leaning back in his chair. "That still leaves plenty of time to evacuate if necessary. Sorry to pull rank on you, Thelma, but the final decision is mine. I say we continue with the regular routine till Jenkins determines what we're actually up against."

"But our responsibility—" Hunnicut began.

"Our responsibility is to pump as much oil as quickly as we can," Maxwell interrupted sternly. "That's what I intend to do." He glanced at Frank, then quickly away again. "Good evening, all."

Frank stepped back to let the lanky Texan leave the room.

"That cowboy is going to get us all killed," Hunnicut muttered just loud enough for Maxwell to hear. Frank was amazed at her nerve in talking back to a higher-up. But Maxwell continued down the stairs, pretending not to hear.

"I guess he knows what he's doing, Thelma," Alvarez said when Maxwell was out of earshot. "But I'm going to work up a flight evac schedule just in case." He turned to his pilots. "Okay, boys, you heard the guy. We're going to have some heavy weather tomorrow. Get a good night's sleep, and I'll see you all here tomorrow morning, five-thirty sharp.''

Frank hadn't seen Maxwell's cutthroat side before. The man's willingness to risk the workers' lives was disturbing. On the other hand, Frank realized he hadn't made any truly dangerous decision—at least not yet. Frank pondered again what Hunnicut might have meant by "any more stupid chances" Lone Star had already taken.

"Hey, Lee." A young, red-haired, freckle-faced pilot stuck out his hand to shake Frank's. "A few of us are going down to the rec room to play cards. Want to come along?''

"Sure," Frank said. This would be a perfect chance to bring up the subject of that day's accident and get a sense of what the other workers suspected was going on. He followed the pilots down the stairs, his mind working out a plan fast. He wanted to know whether any of them had heard of FOE and the disaster ten years ago. He wanted to know if anything had gone wrong with the choppers. And he intended to ask what chances had been taken with the Heron Field crew before.

Sticking his hands in his jacket pockets, he hurried to catch up.

While Frank was playing cards belowdecks, Joe sat at Thelma Hunnicut's metal desk, struggling against a tower of paperwork. The forms he'd been ordered to fill out included everything from food orders for the cafeteria to employment applications from men who'd been hired for the rig.

"No wonder Thelma acts so mad," Joe muttered to himself as he slapped another form facedown on the "finished" pile. "One employee in charge of several hundred men, and nearly all of them needing medicine or special food or a change of room at one time or another." And all Hunnicut had to help her handle Home Base was the troublemaking Purdy. A job like that would make an angry Amazon out of anyone.

"Oh," Joe said out loud as he scanned the next sheet of paper. It was his own employment application—filled out, Joe knew, by Clem Maxwell. The application said that Joe had worked in the mailroom at Lone Star's main office for two years. After that, he'd handled Mr. Baker's business correspondence.

No wonder she gave me all this paper to deal with, Joe thought with a sigh. He put the application in a stack for filing. So far, the other applications had told him plenty about the backgrounds of his fellow workers: most of them were Texans, some working off shore to earn money for college or to buy a house for their families, but no one so far had included the FOE disaster of ten years before in their list of work experience.

Joe decided to try to reach his father on the shortwave radio. The radio sat on a table against the rear wall in Hunnicut's office, so Joe could simply swivel his chair around to operate it. He slipped on the headphones, switched the radio on, and spoke into the microphone: "This is Heron Field calling HQ," he said.

"Heron, this is HQ," crackled a familiar voice over the headset. It was Mr. Baker himself. "That you, Joe?"

Joe grinned. For the first time since he'd gone to work on this case, he felt properly appreciated. "Roger, sir," he said importantly.

"Glad to hear your voice," Baker said. "Your daddy's been worried about you two."

"We thought he might be, sir. Could you tell him we've arrived and we're okay?" Joe asked.

"Tell him yourself," Baker replied. "He's right here."

"Joe?" Fenton's voice sounded faint over the headset. "You're all right?"

"Sure, Dad," Joe said jauntily, leaning back in Hunnicut's chair and beginning to enjoy himself. "I guess you know about the accident on Alpha rig. There was a riot in the cafeteria tonight between the Mexicans and Americans, too, but Frank and I survived. We're starting to think Mr. Baker might be right about the sabotage being linked to the split between the two groups of workers."

51

"Roger," Fenton Hardy answered. "But I have some other news that throws suspicion the other way."

Joe leaned forward. "What's that?"

"Listen carefully—I have to keep this short," his father answered. "My sources in the Bureau tell me they have put a spy in FOE. Now, according to this spy, FOE has someone on Heron Field. Repeat, FOE has an agent on the field. At this point there's no way to know whether the agent's there as a saboteur. But it's possible."

"Roger," Joe said somberly. "Do you have a name?"

"Not yet," Fenton said. "But FOE refers to the person as 'Deep.' "

"Deep?" Joe repeated. "What could that mean?"

"Your guess is as good as mine," Fenton answered.

Joe thought for a moment. "Listen, Dad," he said, "there are a couple of people here who we think seem suspicious. We were hoping you could do a background check on Dave Rubel, Darryl Purdy, and a Mr. Lopez from the Mexican contingent. We especially want to know if Rubel or Purdy was at the FOE disaster ten years ago. If they were, one of them may be the FOE agent. In fact, if you could research that whole disaster, it might give us some leads."

"Yes, sir." Fenton's voice over the wire

sounded impressed. "Now we're going to have to cut this short. Don't—repeat—do *not*—call on the radio unless it's an emergency."

"Why?" Joe asked. "You wanted me to check in every day."

"Listen, Joe. The FOE agent in all probability has a shortwave radio himself. He's keeping in touch with their main organization somehow. If he has a radio, he could be listening to our conversation right now. So take care. Over and out."

The radio went dead. Joe switched it off and removed the headset. Then he leaned back in Thelma Hunnicut's chair, deep in thought.

So Maxwell was right, Joe thought. There was an agent for FOE on Heron Field. He—or she—was known as Deep.

Joe tried to figure out what the cover name meant. It could stand for "deep cover," Joe mused. Possibly it meant that the FOE agent spent a lot of time in the deep, meaning he was a diver like Matt Blaine. Joe nodded. That might explain how they'd managed to detonate that underground explosive.

A diver wouldn't have been able to set up that day's accident, though, Joe reasoned.

*Deep—deep*—Joe turned the word over in his head.

Suddenly he sat up. The name could be a very subtle undercover name. Or it could be very simple.

He crossed the office to a row of filing cabinets on either side of a steel door in the far wall. Joe hadn't gone through the files yet, having wanted to make some progress on his work in case Hunnicut dropped in. But now he opened a drawer marked Personnel: N-Z, and began riffling through the files in the *P* section.

"Deep," he muttered. *D.P.* Those were Darryl Purdy's initials. Joe found the file for Purdy and pulled it from the cabinet. He opened the file to see where Purdy had been ten years previously or to find anything to link him with FOE. . . .

Just then Joe heard footsteps in the corridor. They paused outside the door to the outer office. Someone was out there! Maybe the FOE agent had listened in on Joe's conversation with Fenton. Maybe Joe's cover had been blown.

Hastily Joe returned the file, closed the drawer, and looked around for somewhere to hide. There was no place in the office except under the desk. The first place someone would look, Joe thought.

His eyes fell on a steel door near the filing cabinet. A sign on the door read, Danger! Authorized Personnel Only. Ignoring the sign, Joe tried the knob. The door was locked.

Now what? Joe thought frantically, listening for footsteps. There was no sound. Maybe his ears had been playing tricks on him earlier, he thought. Silently he stepped through the door into the dark outer office. He peered through the shadows. It seemed empty.

Joe heard a sinister *swishhh* coming from the shadows behind him. He half-turned, raising his arm to try to block the oncoming blow.

Too late, he realized as something hard and blunt struck him above the left ear. Bright flashes of light exploded before his eyes, and he collapsed instantly.

# Chapter

## 7

"JOE!" a voice pleaded. "Are you okay?"

Joe Hardy moaned. Through a mist he saw Thelma Hunnicut kneeling over him, her face a picture of shock and concern.

"I think so," Joe said, sitting up. He winced as a sharp pain shot through his head. Then his face lit up. "You called me Joe!"

"What?" Hunnicut said, confused.

"You called me by my name, instead of Blondie." Joe pointed out. He winced again and touched a sore spot on the back of his head. "What happened?"

"You tell me," his boss said, rocking back on her heels. "I didn't know the name Blondie bugged you," she added. "I just called you that as a joke."

"Some joke." Joe got to his feet warily.

"Here." Hunnicut stood up and handed him a towel soaked in ice water. "I was just about to apply first aid. Press this to the back of your head. There's no blood, but you'll have a bump tomorrow morning."

She leaned against the counter while Joe gingerly followed orders. "So who did this to you?" she demanded sharply. "I came up to check on your progress and found you sprawled out here."

"The last thing I remember, I was working in your office," Joe countered, dabbing at his wound. "I heard someone out here. Whoever it was hit me as I came out the door."

"Why would someone attack you?" Hunnicut asked, amazed. "You don't even know anyone yet."

"Beats me." Perhaps it was the FOE agent, or maybe someone who hoped to grab a look at Hunnicut's records. Or else—Joe glanced apprehensively at his boss, who had gone to have a look around the inner office—could Hunnicut have knocked him out herself? Clearly the woman was strong enough to do it.

"Nothing was stolen from the office that I can see," she said, rejoining him at the counter. "How about you? Check your pockets."

"I didn't have anything worth stealing," Joe objected as he turned his pockets inside out. A wallet, a pack of gum, and the key to his cabin tumbled to the floor. "See? Everything's here."

"What about the office key?" Hunnicut asked him.

"You're right," Joe said. "That's gone." He looked at her. "Would someone have knocked me out for that?"

Hunnicut frowned. "There's the storage room in my office," she said slowly.

"You mean the room with the steel door?" he asked, remembering the Danger sign.

"Right. We store things in there that we don't want harmed by the salt air," she told him. "A few important files, our computer software, and—"

Hunnicut's blue eyes widened. "We also keep the explosives used for drilling there," she told Joe. "You don't think—"

She didn't complete the sentence but ran back into the inner office.

Nursing his wound, Joe followed her in time to see her try the steel door's knob.

"Thank goodness, no one had a chance to get in," she said, crossing to a phone on her desk. She pressed a button on the phone and spoke into it. "Maxwell?" she said. "Thelma here. Can you come to my office right away? We have a minor emergency. Right. See you then."

"Who has a key to that room?" Joe asked.

"Only Darryl Purdy, Clem Maxwell, and me," Hunnicut told him. "But now someone has yours."

"I'm sorry," Joe said.

"Don't worry about it," his boss replied. "It's not your fault." She glanced at the piles of paper on her desk. "You made good progress," she admitted. "Now, why don't you go to your cabin and get some rest? We'll set up a watch here tonight, and tomorrow we'll change the locks."

"Okay," Joe said, suddenly reluctant to leave. It was almost ten o'clock, he realized, and he needed to meet Frank at the evac station. "You're sure you'll be okay?"

"No problem, Blondie," his boss said jauntily. Then she blushed. "I mean—Joe."

Joe chuckled as he maneuvered the mazelike corridors and exited onto the catwalk leading to the lifeboat. Being an administrative assistant to Thelma Hunnicut wasn't so bad after all. She came on strong, but Joe guessed anyone would have to, running a place like this. He spotted Frank leaning against the rail by the lifeboat and hurried to join him.

"It's about time," Frank said, checking his watch. "You're ten minutes late."

"Sorry about that," Joe answered casually. "I was attacked by an unknown assailant and left unconscious. I'm okay now," he added, showing Frank the bump on his head and grinning at his brother's shocked reaction. "Thelma helped me keep the swelling down."

"Thelma Hunnicut nursed your wound?" Frank said incredulously. "I don't believe it." Then he frowned. "Who do you think attacked you? What have you been up to, anyway?"

Joe filled Frank in on what had happened

since they'd separated after dinner. Then Frank told his brother about the pilots' meeting and Jenkins's weather report.

"No wonder it's so windy," Joe remarked. "I was wondering if it was always like this."

"I played cards with the other pilots for an hour afterward," Frank continued. "I wanted to get their input on what's been going on at Heron Field."

"What did they say?" Joe asked him.

Frank shrugged. "Not as much as I'd hoped. Apparently, Purdy's not the only one who thinks the project is jinxed. A couple of the guys are looking for new jobs, afraid their choppers will break down in the air and crash."

"Did they say anything about today's accident on Alpha rig?" Joe asked.

"One did. He was the one who ferried the two wounded guys to the hospital in Houston. He saw the damage himself, from the air and from the ground. He says there's no way that broken chain hoist was an accident. He said the chain was just too thick to snap like that. At least I don't think any of them is a FOE agent. They didn't seem at all curious about me—or why I was asking so many questions."

That reminded Joe of the radio conversation he'd had with their father. He filled Frank in on the news concerning the FOE agent.

"He goes by the code name Deep," Frank repeated thoughtfully, turning toward the water and gazing toward the floating platforms. Even at night the rigs were making their ceaseless, monotonous noise. Frank remembered Maxwell telling them that the search for oil never stopped.

"Right." Joe turned toward the Gulf, too. "And I'm willing to bet that Deep stands for someone with the initials *D.P.*"

Frank looked at his brother. "Someone like Darryl Purdy?"

"You've got it," Joe said. "I wouldn't put it past a creep like that to sneak up and hit someone from behind—"

Frank shook his head. "It doesn't make sense. Using someone's initials for his code name is too obvious. Besides, why would Purdy attack you? He already has a key to the office—and a key to the storeroom, for that matter."

"Maybe," Joe said. His attention was distracted just then. "What's that?" he asked, pointing out over the waves.

Frank followed Joe's gaze to an object bobbing on the water a short distance away from the four floating rigs. The object was smaller than any of the platforms, but it was covered with lights.

"It's a boat of some kind," Frank said, interested. "Maybe it's a fishing trawler."

"It's called a standby boat," a voice corrected Frank directly behind them. The Hardys spun around.

"Oh. You surprised us," Joe said, seeing Clem Maxwell standing behind them.

"Sorry about that," Maxwell said. "Just out

for a late-night stroll. I was at the administration office, where I understand somebody really surprised you."

"Do you have any idea who it might be?" Joe asked him.

"You're the detectives," Maxwell reminded Joe. "You're supposed to tell me."

"We have a few suspects," Frank rushed to defend himself and his brother. "We just don't want to discuss them until we've narrowed down our list."

Maxwell frowned. "I sure do hope you narrow it down soon," he said in his thick Texas drawl. "First accidents, now personal attacks on workers. You boys had better speed things up or we're just going to have to close down."

Maxwell's gaze flickered past the Hardys to the water beyond. "That's funny," he said, stepping closer to the rail.

"What is?" Frank asked, turning to look out at the Gulf again.

"The standby boat. It's changed direction."

"So?" Joe asked.

"It's supposed to make a constant circuit of the rigs," Maxwell told them. "Under international law, an independently owned boat is supposed to circle an oil field constantly, ready to help out in case of emergency. But this one's just turning around in the water. It's not doing its job."

"Maybe it's in trouble," Joe suggested.

"Maybe." Maxwell turned to go. "I'll try to

contact the boat by radio," he said. "You boys contact me the minute you think you have that FOE agent nabbed."

The tall, middle-aged Texan left quickly, and Frank and Joe checked out the boat again. "It's reversed direction again. Like they're stalling for time," Joe said.

He rubbed the back of his head thoughtfully. "A boat like that would have perfect access to all four rigs and even this flotel. Maybe I should find out who operates it."

"Good idea," Frank said. "In the morning. Which starts for us at five-thirty sharp."

"Right," Joe said. "You go to your cabin first. I'll follow in a minute. We don't want people to see us together too often. Besides, I need some more fresh air to clear my aching head."

"Gotcha," Frank said. "Good night."

When Frank had left the catwalk, Joe turned back to the standby boat again. It was still carving out a small circle in the waves, making no progress in any direction.

Just then, Joe saw something out of the corner of his eye. He slipped back into the shadows. Slightly above him, at the railing of the flotel's upper deck, was a flash of bright white light. Joe stared until he spotted another flash of light, then another. It was a simple flashlight, he realized. Someone on the top deck was signaling the standby boat!

Joe stepped forward to try to identify the signaler hidden in the shadows on deck. But Joe's foot kicked into something, causing a metallic clang. A metal bucket filled with rivets scattered at his feet. When he looked back up, the dark figure, still unrecognizable, was staring down at him. Then the figure turned and ran, disappearing from view.

Not this time! Joe silently assured the signaler as he raced to the steel ladder that linked the catwalk to the upper deck. He clattered up the steps, but by the time he reached the top the area was empty. Panting for breath, Joe strained his ears for any sound. All he heard were the ocean breeze, the crash of the waves, and the roar of the oil pumps on the distant rigs.

Joe turned back to the standby boat, trying to make out the details of it. He could see people moving about on the boat's deck, but there were no flashes of light in the darkness.

Just then Joe heard a siren start over the flotel's loudspeakers—low at first but earsplitting a second later. "Red alert!" a voice announced over the loudspeaker. "Go to your evac stations! This is not a drill!"

"Another accident?" Joe said out loud, pushing back from the rail. He could hear footsteps running in the distance. He needed to get downstairs.

Joe started to turn, but suddenly he found he couldn't. Someone had approached from behind him, and now a pair of strong arms was wrapped around his waist. Before he knew what was happening, Joe's attacker began lifting him up and over the deck rail.

"Hey!" Joe fought back furiously, but his arms were pinned, and therefore he was helpless. He tried to twist around to get a look at his attacker, but the man stayed directly behind him. Joe screamed, hoping to get the attention of workers racing to their stations, but the noise of the siren drowned him out.

"Go to your evac stations!" the voice on the loudspeaker continued. "This is not a drill!"

Almost four stories below, the black waves of the Gulf crashed against the side of the flotel. Joe stared at the water, struggling mightily for release.

Release was what his attacker gave him. His head ringing with the noise of the siren, Joe felt the man's arms let go. Panicked, Joe grasped wildly for support, but found nothing but air.

"Heeeelp!" Joe yelled as he plummeted through the chill night air. No one could hear him over the scream of the siren, Joe realized. He plunged headfirst toward the roiling waves.

# Chapter

# 8

I'M DROWNING! Joe screamed silently as he plunged beneath the surface of the water. His momentum did slow down, and after an eternity he began rising to the top again. A moment later his head burst through a wave. He gasped wildly for air, spluttering and coughing as another wave washed over him.

"Heeeelp!" Joe shouted, trying to stay afloat. The Gulf in November was cold, and he was afraid he might not survive long. Over the noise of the waves and the siren, Joe thought he heard a faint voice calling "overboard—" There were no more words, and he feared he might have imagined the one.

So this is how it's going to end, he thought morbidly as the siren wailed and the water pulled him slowly back down.

\* \* \*

Frank yawned as he descended the stairs to the flotel's residential section. He was tired and worried, now pretty sure that the FOE agent on board must be involved in the series of accidents. Whoever had stolen Joe's key could be the saboteur and must not already have a copy of the administration office key. That eliminated Darryl Purdy, Thelma Hunnicut, and, Frank guessed, Clem Maxwell as possible suspects. Dave Rubel, with his odd inquisitiveness about Joe and Frank, and Lopez, with his resentment against the Americans, were still on Frank's list.

That's not counting any of the other two hundred ninety-five workers on this project whom we haven't even identified yet, he reminded himself.

Frank was just inserting his key into the lock on his cabin door when the siren went off. Frank yanked the key out of the lock and started running. "Report to evac stations," he heard the voice order over the loudspeaker. His heart pounding, he yanked open the door to the staircase and raced upstairs again.

Frank ran up the stairwell filled with other workers. He outstripped most of them, taking three steps at a time. He pulled open the door leading to the catwalks and ran full speed toward his lifeboat.

Frank was the first person there. "Where's Joe?" he muttered, ripping off the tarp and checking inside the boat. It was empty. Frank searched wildly, half-deafened by the siren.

"Joe!" Frank yelled as several men came running down toward the Hardys' evac station. His attention was caught by something at the edge of the deck above. Frank peered through the darkness, and for an instant he thought he saw a figure leaning far over the railing. Then, in a pause in the announcer's instructions, he heard a fragment of a shout.

"Joe?" Frank yelled, starting toward the steps that led to the upper deck. He ran faster, pushing past several workers who were running the opposite way.

"Hold on, guy!" a worker yelled at Frank as the older Hardy started up the steps just as the worker started down. "There aren't any evac stations above deck. Get back down!"

"Get out of my way!" Frank yelled, pushing past the well-meaning worker. "I have an emergency to get to!"

"Yeah," the worker called after him. "But you're supposed to get to it *downstairs!*"

Frank didn't even hear the warning over the noise of the siren as he ran across the deck to the area where he thought he'd heard Joe. The spot was in deep shadow, but he could just make out some kind of struggle going on.

"Joe!" he yelled as the announcement on the loudspeaker began again. As he approached the fighting pair, one of the bodies was lifted up and out over the water.

"Heeelp!" Frank heard his brother scream as he fell to the water below. With a shout of rage, Frank leapt toward Joe's attacker. The dark figure turned, and Frank saw that his face was hidden by a large bandanna.

"I'll kill you!" Frank shouted, out of control now. He aimed a karate kick straight at the masked attacker's face. The man was too quick for him and pulled a knife and ducked low. A split second later Frank's standing leg flew out from under him and he slammed straight down on the cement floor.

"Wait!" Frank yelled as the masked figure raced out of sight. He struggled to his feet to chase him, but his left leg collapsed in pain. The attacker had slashed the leg to force Frank to fall. Frank ripped off the end of his shirt, bound up the wound, and limped as fast as he could for the stairs.

"Man overboard!" Frank shouted to the small group of men now assembled at the Hardys' evac station. The men peered up at him, unable to make out what he was saying over the noise.

"Man overboard!" Frank limped toward them, pointing wildly toward the water. When the men finally understood him, they rushed to the rail.

"I see him!" one worker shouted as Frank approached them. "Right there, near the platform—see?"

Frank stepped forward and stared in horror at the water. "That's Joe!" he shouted over the siren. "We have to save him!"

"Calm down, man!" one of the other workers shouted back, placing a hand on Frank's shoulder. "We'll get him out."

Frank peered into the darkness until, to his relief, he spotted Joe's head above the surface of the waves. "It's cold down there. He can't last long! No one can hear us over this noise!"

"Look," another of the workers said loudly, leaping into the lifeboat. "This thing's full of life jackets. Throw one down."

Of course. In his panic, Frank realized, he hadn't been thinking clearly. He took the life jacket the worker handed him and tossed it down.

"It's too far from him," shouted the worker beside Frank, peering down. "Throw another one."

This time, the worker in the boat tossed a life jacket directly into the water, without handing it to Frank. Frank watched as the jacket nearly hit Joe in the head. To Frank's relief, Joe swam to the jacket and worked it around his shoulders and under his arms. The jacket would help Joe to stay afloat until they could figure out how to get him out.

"Hey, look," the worker in the lifeboat said. "Flares!"

Before Frank could say a word, the worker had lifted a flare gun out of the lifeboat and jammed a flare into its firing chamber. Frank watched as the man held the gun high above his head and aimed it out to sea. The man pulled the trigger, and with a loud *whoosh* the flare rocketed into the sky. Frank watched the tail of the flare arc over the sea.

"That should do it," shouted the man standing next to Frank. They watched as the flare ignited, lighting the night sky directly above the standby boat. By the flare's crackling glow, Frank could see figures rushing around on the deck of the boat. They were looking toward the flotel. They saw Joe!

Just then the siren cut off. In the silence that followed, Frank watched the standby boat maneuver toward Joe. The workers cheered as someone on deck tossed a large orange life preserver to Joe and started to pull him in. Relief flooded over Frank as Joe was lifted on board.

Someone had tried to kill Joe for a second time, Frank realized. This time he'd almost succeeded. As he turned away from the railing, Frank vowed that it wouldn't happen again.

Joe Hardy was having a dream. It started badly: he was in a roaring, wave-swept sea, struggling to stay afloat.

Suddenly a rope appeared, and Joe clung to it as the waves grew in intensity. He swallowed and was blinded by salt water, the waves now beating over his head. At last, Joe decided to stop struggling. He would simply let go and drift down into the cold darkness, down into oblivion, down into peace. . . .

Instead of drifting down into the ocean and

death, Joe felt himself moving in jerks along the surface of the waves. Then everything went black, until he saw a beautiful, dark-eyed, black-haired angel lean over and gently place her lips on his.

*"Es muerto?"* a harsh, guttural voice asked.

"No, he's not dead," replied a soft, lilting female voice. Joe opened his eyes. Directly above his face was the beautiful angel of his dream. She smiled at him. "He's still with us," she said, speaking with a slight accent.

"Hi," said Joe, his voice still hoarse. "I guess this must be heaven—or that standby boat."

"It isn't heaven," said the harsh masculine voice. Joe sat up and peered around groggily. He was on a cot in the spartan cabin of a boat. A tall, dark-skinned man was standing by the door. He gave Joe a condescending smile. "So, young friend, what made you decide on a moonlight swim?"

"I didn't decide," Joe said, rubbing his head, which still hurt from the impact of his fall and his earlier adventure. "I was pushed. By the man who was signaling to you. At least, I guess that's who it was. The guy sneaked up on me from behind."

"Signaling to us?" The man frowned at Joe. "I don't understand you. There were no signals."

"Sure there were," Joe insisted. "He was signaling from the top deck of the flotel. I saw it with my own eyes, so don't bother denying it. Just tell me what he was signaling about.''

"This is ridiculous," the man snapped at the woman, losing his temper. "A drill casing blows apart, and we waste our time with this boy! I told you we should have left him for the flotel to save, Maria.''

"We couldn't leave him floating there, Hector," the woman protested. "The water is cold. He could have drowned!''

"Let the flotel take care of its own." The man turned to go. "Our job is to watch the rigs and deal with emergencies—not to baby-sit foolish *children!''*

The man started to leave the room, but Joe was too near the end of his rope to let himself be pushed around. "Someone was flashing signals!" he yelled after Hector's departing back, sitting up on the cot despite Maria's restraining hand. "I say there's a spy on board this boat! And if it isn't you, then you know who it is, and what he's here for! Maybe this entire boat is owned by FOE!''

At this, Hector froze midstep. Joe watched, breathing deeply, as the man slowly turned around to face him again. Joe noticed Maria shrink back as Hector glowered at Joe from beneath thick black brows.

"Enrique! Carlos!" Hector shouted, keeping his eyes on Joe. Instantly two burly men entered the room.

Hector gave them an order in Spanish, and

73

they moved toward Joe, each grasping one of his arms. Joe struggled, but was too weakened by his ordeal to break their hold.

"Relax, *hombres*," Joe said feebly. He turned to Maria. "I thought this was supposed to be a rescue."

"Hector!" Maria pleaded.

"Don't be stupid, Maria," Hector responded. "This worm has questioned our honesty." He turned to his two men. "Throw him back into the ocean to try his luck with the sharks!"

# Chapter

## 9

JOE STRUGGLED to break the grip of the two men, but his strength was sapped. He looked from Maria to Hector and back again. Suddenly Maria stepped forward.

"Oh, go soak that hot head of yours!" she snapped at Hector. She turned to the men holding Joe and spoke commandingly to them in Spanish. The two men released Joe.

"Thanks," Joe said, flexing his biceps. He suppressed a grin, seeing how easily tiny Maria had cowed these vicious-looking men. "If it's all the same to you guys," he couldn't resist adding, "I've had enough swimming for one night."

"Please excuse my brother Hector." Maria turned to Joe with an apologetic smile. "He felt that you were insulting him. He sometimes lets his temper rule his head."

"No hard feelings," Joe said, holding out his hand to Hector. Hector scowled, but grudgingly did shake Joe's hand.

"I didn't mean to insult you," Joe said. "But I swear, I saw someone signaling. You didn't notice it yourself?"

"We were focused on the emergency," Maria told him. "A terrible tragedy—for Lone Star and PetroMex both. Someone put a bomb of some kind in the drilling mud. It exploded in the well under the sea."

"Drilling mud?" Joe asked. Then he remembered Maxwell explaining that mud was pumped into the drilling pipe under pressure to force the drill farther down beneath the ocean floor. If a bomb had been dropped into the mud and sent down the pipe, it would have destroyed the casing around the bit and forced the workers to stop drilling.

"They will have to fish for the bit, which is now broken off," Hector told him. "It could take days—or weeks."

"That's terrible." Joe wondered what Maxwell would say. Then he wondered, again, what the standby boat had been doing going in circles in the water while someone was signaling from Home Base. Could someone on this boat have caused the explosion—maneuvering close to Delta rig after sundown and slipping a small explosion into the drilling mud?

He wanted to ask Maria more questions, but

just then a voice from outside the cabin called, "Ahoy!"

"We are at the ladder," Hector said.

"Believe me, we mean no harm to the rigs or any of the men on them," Maria said. "Please—promise me you will not report what you have seen tonight."

"Well, I—" Joe stared into the woman's brown eyes and forgot what he was going to say.

"Come." Hector signaled to his two men, who helped Joe to his feet—gently, this time. "It is time to go."

The two men released Joe on the deck of the standby boat as it pulled alongside one of the submarines supporting HomeBase. A ladder led from just above the water's surface to the top deck of the flotel. Joe gripped the slick, salt-encrusted bottom rung of the ladder. With the two men's help, he hauled himself up and began the long climb to the deck of HomeBase.

"Joe—are you all right?" Thelma Hunnicut stood on the deck of HomeBase as Joe pulled himself up over the edge.

"I'll survive," Joe said. He saw that Frank and Clem Maxwell were standing with Hunnicut.

"What happened, son?" Maxwell asked. "Were you pushed?"

"Of course he was pushed!" Frank snapped, exasperated. "I told you—I saw it happen!"

"Er—actually," Joe stammered, remembering Maria's request, "I, uh— Well, actually, I slipped."

"You what?" Frank stared at his brother. He started to argue. Then abruptly he shut his mouth. Joe must have his reasons.

Hunnicut was not so easily silenced. "First someone conks you over the head in my office, then you slip off the flotel? I tell you, Clem," she said, slapping Joe's back a little too hard, "this one's a real adventurer. All right, go to bed, kid, and I mean it this time." She bent toward him, murmuring in his ear, "And I want the *real* story tomorrow."

Weary and annoyed, Hunnicut and Maxwell told the boys good night and left. As soon as they were alone, Frank asked Joe, "What's the scoop? Why wouldn't you admit that someone dunked you?"

"I promised someone I wouldn't tell."

"You what? Who?" Frank demanded.

"Someone on the standby boat."

"You're kidding!" Frank's incredulous look switched suddenly to understanding. "Right," he said. "I bet she's pretty cute."

"She is," Joe admitted. "But I also trust her. She's the only one who cared if I survived. So tell me—how did Maxwell take the news of Delta rig's explosion?"

"He nearly exploded himself," Frank said grimly, leading the way below. "He told me—before Hunnicut showed up—that he wants that FOE agent identified and arrested tomorrow. I guess his job's on the line here. Otherwise he wouldn't be so panicked."

Joe told his brother about somebody signaling the standby boat. Then he listened to Frank's account of his struggle with the man who had pushed Joe overboard. "Did you get a look at him?" Joe asked.

"All I know is, he's over six feet tall and left-handed. He cut my leg with a knife. It's really not more than a bad scratch—so don't worry. From what I could see the knife might have been a steak knife from the cafeteria."

"A steak knife. Great," Joe said. "Anyone could have one of those. Maybe Lopez—"

"That's what I was thinking," Frank agreed. "The attacker did have Lopez's build. Anyway, tomorrow try to go through the employee files for the names of everyone over six feet tall."

"Oh, sure," Joe said glumly. "I'll add that to my list of things to do. Just think, we have all of twenty-four more hours to find the culprit and hand him over to the boss."

Dawn was breaking as Frank crossed the helipad to the flight control room the next morning. In the distance he saw the four rigs, only three of them operating now, and one of those three sporting a gash in its side.

He entered the flight control office to find Alvarez standing in the middle of the cramped room, his group of young pilots around him.

"Morning, Frank," Alvarez said as several of the pilots gave the rookie a grin and a nod. "You're just in time. I'm handing out assignments. Here's your schedule,'' he said, handing Frank a clipboard.

Frank checked the computer printout clipped to it. "What about the hurricane?" he asked.

Alvarez frowned. "Jenkins just reported that our nasty weather has been upgraded from a gale to a tropical storm and is still heading our way. Looks like it'll be a hurricane, all right. I'm sending for a fleet of Chinooks from the mainland. We'll probably evacuate Heron Field this evening. In the meantime"—he shrugged—"be careful."

Careful is right, Frank realized. Once word got out that the rigs were to be evacuated, the saboteur would know he had just a few hours left to act. Who knew what an environmental terrorist could do to a rig when cornered? Frank, for one, hoped he'd never have to know.

Frank and the other pilots strode out into the stiff morning breeze. Frank cheered up when he spotted the twelve-seater Bell 212 choppers being wheeled out to each helipad. Already, lines of Blue shift workers were waiting for the pilots to take them to their jobs—just like commuters waiting for a bus.

Seven men waited to board Frank's chopper. Frank spotted Joe among them, toting a large canvas duffel bag. Nodding briefly to Joe, as though he barely knew him, Frank yelled out, "Okay, guys. Next stop, Alpha rig!"

The men clambered in as Frank ran through

his preflight checks. As if by chance, Joe took the seat nearest the pilot. Frank glanced at his brother and the duffel. "I see by my schedule that that must be freight for Deep Six," he said.

"Yeah," Joe replied. "It's electronic equipment. I guess it's important. Purdy said they wanted it hand delivered."

As Joe buckled himself in Frank fired up the engines. The rotors shuddered and groaned to life. Soon the vibration of the spinning blades shook the entire chopper. Frank was cleared for takeoff, and the chopper lifted effortlessly into the air.

Frank enjoyed flying toward the rigs in the buffeting winds. In real life, the chopper handled sharply, providing a challenge no simulator could match. The nearest rig—Alpha—was about five hundred yards from HomeBase. After dropping off a construction foreman there, Frank piloted the chopper southwest a quarter of a mile to Beta rig and dropped off five more passengers.

Only Frank and Joe remained to continue to Deep Six, the next stop. Raindrops spattered the chopper's windscreen. He glanced at his brother. "Did you find anything in Hunnicut's files this morning?"

"I didn't get a chance," Joe told him. "Purdy sent me on this errand the minute I got to the office."

"It looks like we'll be evacuating soon, because

of the weather,'' Frank warned him. ''That means we have only a few hours—not 24—to crack the case.''

Alvarez's voice crackled over Frank's headset. ''Attention, Flight 02 Gamma Delta—this is Control,'' he said. ''The heavy weather seems to be picking up. All flights are grounded while we wait to see if this thing blows over. Wait on Deep Six for further instructions.''

''Roger.'' Frank peered through the windscreen. The landing pad of Deep Six was nearly hidden by fog. Slowly and carefully Frank worked the controls. Finally the chopper landed with a thud.

''Wow,'' Joe said, unbuckling his seat belt. ''This place looks great.''

Frank peered out through the mist at the strange-looking ship. It resembled a huge catamaran mounted on two submarines. The deck was fifty yards long and twenty yards wide, and crowded with steel tanks, drums, and long pipelines. Two corrugated metal buildings stood on the deck. The larger one abutted a gap in the center of the boat.

''That must house the saturation tank where the divers live,'' said Joe. ''A guy on the chopper from Houston told me all about it.''

Frank watched the ground crew strap the chopper's pontoons to the deck. ''I'm stuck here until further notice,'' he said. ''Mind if I tag along while you deliver your package?''

''Let's go,'' Joe replied.

\*　　\*　　\*

Frank followed Joe into Deep Six's small control room and stared, impressed, at the high-tech equipment installed there. Four men sat at various control panels, monitoring glowing computer screens. The oldest turned to the Hardys as they entered.

"You're from HomeBase?" he asked. "My name's Jordan. I'm skipper of Deep Six."

"Hi," Joe said, holding up the duffel bag. "Here's your delivery from off shore."

"Be careful with that," Jordan barked, taking the bag from Joe. "Reynolds," he said to one of the men staring at a video screen, "the divers' new receivers are here."

"Excellent," the man said. "You hear that, Blaine?" he added into a tiny microphone attached to the headset. "The new squawk boxes are here. Now you have no more excuses for going silent on me."

"Maybe I just like a little peace and quiet, Reynolds," crackled a voice over a speaker near the monitor. Joe moved closer to the screen, peering over the operator's shoulder. "Blaine," he repeated in a low voice to Frank. "That's the guy I told you about. The one next to me on the chopper from Houston who told me about this place."

As Jordan joined the Hardys, Frank spotted the image of a man in a deep-sea diving suit on the screen. The diver was standing on the ocean floor next to what looked like a huge steel drum and had a large sack hanging over his shoulder.

"Yeah, that's Blaine," Jordan said to Frank and Joe. "He's working on the pipeline that carries the crude oil back to Mexico."

"He's five hundred feet below us, right?" Joe asked.

"Right," Jordan replied. "Up here, the wind's blowing at nearly a force four gale—as you know." He nodded to Frank. "Down there, it's as calm as a day in June."

"Who's taking the picture?" Frank asked. "Is there a camera on the diving bell?"

Jordan shook his head. "The diver is about two hundred feet from the diving bell. He's connected to it by a lifeline. We're monitoring him through an ROV with a camera."

"ROV?" Joe asked.

"That stands for Remotely Operated Vehicle. It's a deep-sea drone that follows the diver around. It's connected by cable directly to the control room here." Jordan nodded toward the control panel. Frank saw that Reynolds was operating a joystick, occasionally flicking it a fraction of an inch.

On the screen Blaine hauled the huge bag toward the pipeline. Frank saw a ragged crack in the concrete base underneath. He watched Blaine struggle to fit the bag on top of a pile of other bags already stacked inside the crevice.

"That's quick-drying cement," Jordan said.

"The seabed shifts often around here, and we have to repair the base of the pipeline."

Just then the speaker near the video screen started crackling.

"Reynolds," Blaine's voice cried over the speaker, interrupted by a burst of static.

"I read you, Blaine," Reynolds replied, adjusting several knobs. "What's wrong?"

"This crack wasn't caused by a shift in the seabed," said the voice over the speaker.

"What do you mean?" Reynolds demanded, glancing at the skipper. Frank leaned closer to peer at Blaine's tiny image on the screen.

"It's not a crack," Blaine repeated. "It looks like someone dragged an anchor directly over the pipeline. We're lucky it wasn't ruptured."

Frank glanced at his brother. Who could have dragged an anchor over the pipeline? he wondered. Instantly, he knew the answer.

The only boat he and Joe had seen the night before anywhere near the oil field was the standby boat Joe had been on. Frank remembered Joe's description of the signal lights, and wondered if the two were connected. A man signals a boat with a flashlight, he said to himself. A boat goes around in circles when it's supposed to be cruising the rigs. The boat is manned by a Mexican crew, and the Mexican workers are angry.

Joe had turned an odd shade of green. Things don't look good for the standby boat's crew,

Frank silently told him. No matter how cute they are.

Just then Deep Six lurched forward violently. With a cry, Joe lost his balance and fell to the floor. The lights in the control room went out, and the red glare of an emergency light filled the room.

"To your posts!" Jordan yelled, staggering to the hatch and slapping a button on the wall. A loud siren split the air, and Jordan leaned toward a speaker on the wall. "Mayday! Mayday!" he called. "DPS has cut out! Condition Blue! Condition Blue!"

Frank and Joe moved out of the way as the other men—including Reynolds—scrambled to a bank of controls at the far end of the room. Frank watched as they frantically threw switches and turned knobs and called out readings to one another. Again, the ship lurched.

"Look—the screen's blanked out," Joe said, nodding toward Reynolds's video screen. Blaine's image had disappeared, replaced by snowy static.

A moment later the boat began to stabilize, and Frank watched the picture on the screen clear. He and Joe squinted at the grainy image, relieved when it came into sharper focus.

"It's Blaine," Joe said, moving back toward the screen. Frank moved closer, too, when he realized what had happened. The diver's leg was pinned beneath a pile of three cement bags that had tumbled from beneath the pipeline.

His arms flailed wildly, trying to reach his life-line to the diving bell. But the line trailed wildly before Blaine's face, spewing bubbles into the air.

Frank stared in horror. The lifeline had snapped in two. Blaine was trapped on the ocean floor!

# Chapter

## 10

JOE SLID into the chair at the control panel and grabbed the headset.

"Blaine!" he cried into the microphone. "Can you hear me?"

"Yes," came the faint response over the speaker. "I've switched over to my bailout system. I have enough air for about six minutes. But—my leg—I'm stuck."

"Hold on, Blaine," Joe said into the microphone, keeping his voice steady.

Joe grabbed the joystick and pressed it forward. Blaine's image on the screen seemed to grow larger as the ROV moved forward.

"Blaine," Joe called, "I'm bringing the drone toward you."

"I see it," said Blaine. "Don't come straight for me. You'll crush me against the pipeline."

Beads of sweat formed on Joe Hardy's forehead. He jerked the joystick a bit to the right. The ROV swiveled in that direction. Blaine disappeared from view.

"Too far," said Blaine. "You're heading out of my reach."

Joe moved the joystick a bit to the left, correcting the ROV's path.

"Good," Blaine said. Joe could hear his labored breathing over the speaker. "I should be able to reach it. Don't crash, though!"

The pipeline loomed larger and larger on the monitor as Joe moved the ROV closer. "About ten feet now," Blaine said.

"Hold on!" said Reynolds, returning to his spot and grabbing Joe's shoulder. "The ship is stable. Let me take over."

"Don't jostle the joystick," Joe heard his brother retort. "The ROV is very close to Blaine."

As others gathered around the video screen, Jordan looked at Joe and nodded nervously. "He has it under control," Jordan said. "I hope."

"Slow down," Blaine called over the speaker. Joe pulled back on the joystick. "I can almost reach it," Blaine said. "You're just—out of—my reach . . ."

The image on the screen bobbed wildly.

"Got it," Blaine said. "Stop moving!"

Joe pulled back again on the joystick. The image on the screen was now still. "How are we doing, Blaine?'' he asked. There was no response. ''Blaine?'' Joe cried.

''Still here,'' came the faint voice. ''I'm just thinking about how much this is going to hurt. Okay, I have hold of the under-grid of the ROV. I think she can tow me along without tangling me up in her propellers. Put her into reverse. Gently. Then swing around and take me back to the bell.''

''Roger.'' Joe tapped gingerly on the front of the joystick, thrusting the ROV gently into reverse. Blaine's muted groan came over the speaker. Joe tapped some more. The picture bobbed, but didn't change otherwise. Blaine was still stuck.

Joe swallowed hard. ''I'll have to use more thrust,'' he muttered. He pulled back once on the joystick. Blaine screamed as the ROV moved sharply away from the pipeline.

''Are you all right?'' Joe called as he steadied the joystick. ''Blaine! Can you hear me?''

There was a moment of silence.

''I'm free, anyway,'' Blaine responded in a strangled voice. ''My ankle may be broken. Get me home. Please.''

As the other operators watched intently, Joe gripped the joystick. ''I'm going to turn you around now,'' he said, tilting the stick to the right. The camera panned off the pipeline, into the inky blackness of the vast underwater Gulf. A few fish passed in front of the camera. Then, in the distance, Joe could make out a globular shape. The diving bell.

As Joe operated the joystick, the blurry shape on the screen grew more distinct. Soon it filled the screen. A metallic clang resounded over the speaker as the two crafts hit.

"Door-to-door service," came the faint voice over the speaker. "We made it. Thanks."

Joe let go of the joystick, sat back, and sighed. Behind him, loud cheering filled the room. He turned and saw Frank and the others gathered behind him.

"Great work, kid!" Reynolds said.

Joe grinned sheepishly. "I guess all those hours playing video games finally paid off," he said.

"I can't understand it," Jordan said with a frown. It was five minutes later, and Deep Six had at last been fully stabilized. Blaine was safely in the bell, which was being prepared to come back to the surface. Soon another diver would go down to finish repairing the pipeline.

"We have two computers monitoring the DPS," Jordan said. "How could they both crash at the same time?"

The Hardys stood beside Jordan in a small room called the computer center, adjacent to the control room. Frank gazed along with Jordan into an amber computer screen. "What's DPS?" Frank asked.

"Dynamic Positioning System," Jordan answered. "When a diver is working below, the ship has to stay as steady as a rock. If it doesn't—well, you saw what can happen. To keep the ship steady, there is a series of nine propulsion thrusters on the pontoons. The thrusters can be turned to any angle. One computer system monitors the currents and winds, and positions the thrusters to counteract the motion of the ship. That keeps us steady. The second computer system monitors the first one as a backup. But today, in the middle of a gale, both systems shut down!" Jordan shook his head.

"Could they have been sabotaged?" Frank asked.

Jordan turned and stared at him. "Perhaps," he said slowly. "But it's not like dropping a monkey wrench into a gear box. The saboteur would have to be pretty bright."

"Bright enough to drop a bomb into a vat of drilling mud?" Joe said impulsively. "Or to file down a link in a chain hoist?"

Startled, Jordan looked from Frank to Joe. "You two sure are asking a lot of questions," he said suspiciously. "Who are you, anyway? Did Maxwell send you here?"

"What are you talking about?" Frank said nervously. "We just started working here yesterday."

"Is that right?" Jordan took a step back from the computer screen, moving toward the door leading to the control room. "Working as what? Spies for Maxwell?" He took another step back. "I'm not going to be made a scapegoat for Lone Star's bad luck," he said, raising his voice. "There are no saboteurs on my crew. You go back and tell Maxwell that, you hear?"

"Calm down, Skipper," Joe said. "We didn't mean to—"

"And one more thing," the skipper interrupted as several operators in the next room looked up, startled by the noise. "Tell Maxwell that next time he's too scared to confront me after losing a shouting match, he should find someone besides a couple of kids to do his dirty work!"

"What shouting match?" Frank asked.

"The one we had this morning," Jordan retorted angrily. "Maxwell tried to shut down our operation today. He claimed the weather was too rough. But it's lucky we ignored him and found that damage. If those pipes aren't securely supported when the hurricane hits, they could rupture and we'd have a first-class disaster on our hands."

"You argued over the radio?" Frank asked.

"No. He came out here himself."

Frank and Joe looked at one another, stunned.

"Maxwell was here?" Joe repeated. "When?"

"About five-thirty," Jordan snapped. "He flew himself in one of the Bells. He was waiting for me here when I relieved the night watch."

Frank shook his head. It didn't make sense.

93

Maxwell was willing to work in the face of a hurricane to keep the project going, but he'd wanted to shut down Deep Six for no reason. Frank heard his brother say, "Thanks, Skipper. We're sorry if we stepped on any toes. We don't work for Maxwell—at least not as spies."

The rain had stopped and the wind abated when Frank and Joe returned to the deck of Deep Six, but the waves still crashed nearby. Frank walked to the helipad in silence, thinking about Clem Maxwell. Why would the man in charge of the entire operation do such a bad job of running it?

Frank shook his head, trying to dismiss the images that crowded his mind: of Lopez signaling the standby boat, and the standby boat's crew dragging an anchor over the pipeline, and Darryl Purdy baiting the Mexican workers. . . . He wished they were back on HomeBase so they could contact their father. By now Fenton Hardy must have some leads.

"Next stop is Delta rig," Frank said to his brother as they climbed into the chopper's pilot and copilot seats.

"Purdy told me to pick up the reports on the explosion there," Joe said.

Frank nodded, checking his computer printout. "That's weird," he said. "I'm supposed to pick up another passenger here. No one's around."

Just then the radio crackled to life.

"Gamma Delta 02—do you read?" came Alvarez's voice. Frank grabbed his microphone.

"Lee here," he said.

"You're clear to fly now," replied Alvarez. "We don't know how long the weather will hold, so finish your rounds fast and then hightail it back here."

"Roger," Frank said. "I have a problem, though. One of my passengers is missing. I was supposed to take him to Delta rig."

There was a momentary pause. "That wouldn't be Thelma's boy, would it?" Alvarez asked.

"Thelma's boy?" Joe groaned. "Tell him it's Joe! And I'm right here, on the job!"

"Sorry about that," Alvarez said when Frank, laughing, repeated the message. "She told me to keep an eye on Blondie. Let me check the records."

Frank smiled as his brother fumed.

"The missing passenger is Dave Rubel," Alvarez said. Frank and Joe looked at each other. "He's in equipment maintenance—a computer troubleshooter. He was running an inspection on Deep Six this morning."

Frank looked at his brother. "The DPS?" he asked excitedly.

"It doesn't say here," Alvarez replied. "Anyway, you can't wait for him. He can take the next chopper—if there is one. Go ahead to Delta."

"Roger," Frank said. He buckled his seat belt and reached for the controls.

"Maybe I should stay here and look for Rubel," Joe suggested.

"No," Frank said as he fired up the engine. "If he is the saboteur, he's already made his attempt on Deep Six and failed. Besides, just because he's here doesn't make him that much more of a suspect. A virus could have been placed in the computer weeks or months ago, set to go off when the weather conditions got this choppy."

"Purdy could have done it," Joe said as the helicopter rose into the air. "He's a bright guy, beneath that lizardlike exterior."

Frank hesitated. "Actually," he said, "I'm beginning to have second thoughts about Clem Maxwell."

"Maxwell?" Joe gazed through the windscreen at Delta rig in the distance. "You mean because he was at Deep Six this morning?"

"It's possible," Frank said. "Plus, he's doing everything he can to put these rigs at risk. It just doesn't fit in with the responsible-manager act he gave us back at Lone Star headquarters." Frank aimed the helicopter at Delta rig's helipad, which was still intact. "He's up to something."

Joe shook his head. "You've been breathing too much salt air, Frank. Of course Maxwell's been taking risks. You have to in the oil business. I'd put my money on Darryl Purdy. That guy's been acting fishy."

Just then Joe felt a cold, faint, prickling sensation against the back of his skull.

"Fishy, huh?" said a voice in his ear. "In what way exactly?"

Joe froze, staring straight ahead through the windscreen. "Rubel," he said.

"Bingo." Rubel nudged the tip of the knife closer to Joe's throat. "But my friends just call me Deep."

# Chapter

## 11

FRANK STARED straight ahead. One false move and Joe's life would be over. Frank reached slowly toward the controls to bring the helicopter down to Delta rig.

"Keep flying," Rubel shouted at him, "or I slice this knife across his throat!"

Frank snatched his hand from the controls. "Be cool, Rubel," he said. "Just tell us what the problem is."

"What the problem is?" Rubel struggled with his anger for a moment, and Frank tensed, ready for a fight. Rubel continued, "I was waiting in the chopper for my ride. When I saw you were the pilot, I ducked down, kind of on the spur of the moment. I've had my doubts about both of you since you walked in front of my cycle in Houston. I mean, look at you!

You're not oilmen. What are you—freelance goons the company hired to keep us laborers in line?"

"You're calling *us* goons?" Joe sputtered. At the touch of the knife, though, he fell silent.

"You shut up!" Rubel said to Joe. "I'm talking to the other one." He turned back to Frank. "Tell me who you really are—now—or your friend here gets it," he threatened.

Frank's eyes flicked over to his brother. Joe had broken out in a sweat, and his eyes were closed. Frank knew there was no choice but to come clean. "We're private investigators," he said. "We were hired to keep an eye on things—after all the accidents started to happen."

"Investigators?" Rubel leaned forward, incredulous. "You guys are kids! Who would hire you?"

"We have one or two job skills," Joe said.

"Such as?" Rubel said with a smirk as he lowered his knife.

Out of the corner of his eye, Frank saw Rubel glance over at Joe. In that moment Frank pulled back hard on the controls, lifting the nose of the chopper sharply into the air. The force of the climb knocked Rubel back into his seat.

"Such as this!" Joe spun around and threw a crisp right cross to Rubel's chin.

"Yeow," Joe said, rubbing his fist. "The clown's beard skinned my knuckles."

"Is he out?" Frank asked as he straightened out the chopper's flight path. Joe peered back at the now groggy man.

"Not quite," Joe said, leaning back to pick Rubel's knife up off the floor. "This one's not a steak knife," he told his brother. "It's a switchblade. But he still might be the one who cut you last night."

"Frisk him for ID," Frank replied.

Joe leaned over and jerked a wallet from Rubel's rear pocket. He took out a driver's license and read aloud, " 'Dave Rubel. Resident of the state of Texas.' " Joe peeked over his shoulder at his attacker, who was just returning to his senses. "Boy, for an ugly guy, you sure take a lousy picture."

"For a kid, you pack a punch," Rubel said, rubbing his chin. "I guess a guy needs plenty of muscle to impose Maxwell's will on the Mexicans."

"Don't be stupid," Frank snapped. "We're not imposing anyone's will on anyone else—which is more than I can say for your organization."

"What do you mean?" Rubel asked.

"He means FOE, Rubel," Joe said impatiently. "You know—terrorist tactics in the name of environmental protection? Oil wells blowing up, chain hoists breaking, workers getting sent to the hospital? We know you're a member of FOE. Our source told us the contact's name is Deep."

"Hey, wait a minute," Rubel said angrily. "FOE is opposed to violence, no matter what the situation! I know they used to condone a little guerrilla warfare in the extreme cases," he added when Joe gave him a stern look, "but nothing like that has happened for years. I'm here for the same reason you say you are—to keep an eye on things and try to make sure a disaster doesn't happen."

"Then why attack us?" Joe demanded.

"You were my prime suspects. I was almost positive *you* guys were the saboteurs."

"Hmm." Joe thought this over. "Let's say we believe you," he said. "But then, if *you're* not the saboteur, and *we're* not saboteurs, who—"

"We'll be landing in a minute," Frank said, interrupting Joe. "We have to decide what to do with him."

Joe appeared to think this over. "I guess we should turn him over to Maxwell," he said to Frank. "Even if he didn't sabotage any of the rigs, he's still working here under false pretenses. And he *did* threaten to cut my throat."

"Why turn me in when we can pool our resources?" Rubel asked.

"Well . . ." Joe pretended to be skeptical, but he was pleased at how quickly Rubel had taken the bait.

"Listen," Rubel said. "I've been keeping an eye on some of the Mexican workers. They resent Lone Star's operating in their territory, and they all hate Darryl Purdy's guts. Did you know that the fellow called Juan Lopez is the leader of a radical Mexican workers' union?''

Joe was impressed. "That's why the other workers follow his orders."

"Exactly," Rubel replied as Frank dropped the helicopter toward Delta rig's landing pad. "So what do you say? Allies for the environment? None of us wants an oil spill."

Frank glanced at his brother.

"Agreed," Joe said reluctantly. After the helicopter landed, Joe turned all the way around to shake hands with Rubel. The Texan had already flung open his door and slipped out of the chopper.

"He's getting away!" Joe opened his own door, ready to pursue him across the helipad.

Frank grabbed his brother's wrist. "If you catch up to him," Frank said, "don't turn him in."

"Why not?" Joe asked.

"Because." Frank glanced at the ground crew approaching the chopper with a large handcart. He lowered his voice. "Until we know for sure who to trust around here, we keep all information to ourselves."

Joe shrugged in agreement, and took off after Rubel. Frank started to follow, but one of the ground crew knocked on his window and asked, "You have some heavy freight from HomeBase?"

"It's in the hold," Frank said, distracted.

"That's what I like. A speedy delivery," the man said, opening the door to the freight hold.

Frank gave up the idea of catching up with Joe and joined the ground crew. "What is this?" he asked as the men pulled out a large wooden crate.

"Our new drill bit," the man said. "Now all we have to do is wait till they fish out the old one."

Frank helped load the crate onto the cart. "You guys wouldn't have any idea who might have slipped in that bomb, do you?" he asked, trying to sound casual.

The workers glanced at one another. "Sure don't," the worker Frank had spoken to said. "Wish we did, though. If this field closes down, my family won't have a very happy Christmas."

"Rubel!" Joe heard his voice echo across the platform as he raced toward the ocean side of the helipad. Delta rig had been shut down since the underground explosion, and compared to the other platforms it was eerily quiet. Joe had seen Rubel run to the edge of the platform and disappear. When he arrived at the place he'd last seen him, Joe found nothing but a ladder.

"Here goes nothing," Joe muttered, throwing a leg over the top of the ladder and starting to descend. Forty feet down, the ladder passed a narrow scaffolding that ringed the entire platform. Other scaffoldings were connected to it and crossed under the bottom of the oil rig. Joe guessed that the scaffoldings were used by men painting the rig's underside to keep it from rusting in the salt spray.

"Rubel!" Joe shouted again, knowing he wouldn't answer. He scrambled onto the scaffolding, following one of the paths until he stood near the center of the underside of the rig. From there, looking up through a hole in the platform, Joe could see all the way to the top of the metal tower. Until the night before, a series of metal shafts had led from the underwater oil well to the top of the rig, ready to release oil from the ocean's depths. Now a thick cable hung through the hole on a pulley and chain like the one that had snapped on Alpha rig. Joe saw that the workers were actually fishing for the lost bit at the bottom of the well.

Then he spotted something else. It was Rubel, moving carefully around the platform's perimeter, checking out the sea. As Joe watched, Rubel brought a pair of binoculars up to his eyes. On the horizon Joe saw the standby boat circling the rig.

He's spying on the standby crew, Joe realized. Did Rubel suspect the Mexican crew of working in partnership with Lopez—or was Rubel their partner?

Joe was distracted by the earsplitting whine of metal twisting under stress, and a crashing snap from above the rig.

"Heads up!" someone shouted.

Joe raised his eyes and saw in an instant that the steel cable the workers had been using to fish had slipped from the hoist atop the derrick. As Joe stared in horror, the cable crashed through the gap in the platform floor.

"No!" Joe shouted, backing up. The unthreaded end of the heavy cable was hurtling directly at him!

# Chapter

# 12

"HEEELP!" Joe vaulted over the railing of the wooden scaffolding moments before the steel cable crashed into the spot where he had stood. Dangling from the railing, Joe held on as the entire length of steel cable slithered through the gaping hole it had made to the sea below.

Joe tried to pull himself back up onto the walkway, but his weight caused the railing to creak ominously.

"Come on, don't collapse on me now," Joe muttered as the entire length of scaffolding began to inch toward the water. He realized that the shock of the crash, plus the weight of the cable still on the floor, were proving too much for the walkway to bear.

"Just give me a second," Joe pleaded. He checked frantically to his right, reckoning how long it would take him to inch his way to a stronger walkway twenty yards away. Too long, but Joe had no choice. Holding his breath, he moved hand over hand along the railing.

The end of the scaffolding he had just been holding on to collapsed all at once. Joe hung on to the railing, which now swung free. He tried to pull himself up the rail for better support when the rail snapped in two.

"Whooooa!" Joe yelled as he fell backward toward the sea.

It was a shock when he stopped falling all at once, dangling upside down in midair. His pants leg had caught on the jagged end of the scaffolding that had torn loose.

"Hold on! I'm coming, Joe," he heard a voice call out. Dave Rubel appeared, upside down, in his field of vision. Joe watched as Rubel inched carefully along the scaffolding toward the broken end. With each step, the walkway groaned and sank a little lower toward the sea.

"Watch out," Joe yelled. "It's going to break off completely!"

"I've got you." Rubel knelt near the free end of the walkway and grabbed Joe's leg. Using all his strength, Rubel slowly hauled Joe up without dislodging the scaffolding. Joe could see the muscles bulging beneath the man's T-shirt. A moment later Rubel stopped to catch his breath. Joe watched, upside down, as he looked up toward the top of the platform.

"Hey!" Rubel yelled. "Anyone up there want to give us a hand?"

"Hold on." Joe heard distant voices and the clatter of footsteps on the platform above them. Heads peered over the edge. One of them, Joe recognized despite the blood rushing to his head and nearly blinding him, was Frank.

Ten minutes later Joe sat in the control room of Delta rig, glancing down at his bandaged leg. It was really nothing more than a few scratches. He was lucky.

"Rubel, you're strange," Joe heard Frank say. "One minute you're threatening to slit Joe's throat and the next you're saving his life."

"That's because back then I believed he was a threat to the environment," Rubel said stubbornly. "The second time I knew he was just a dumb kid in the wrong place at the wrong time. FOE members are sworn to protect human life, too, you know."

"A dumb kid?" Joe sputtered. "I wouldn't have even been there, Rubel, if it hadn't been for—"

Just then the office door swung open and Joe abruptly shut his mouth. Joe, Frank, and Rubel turned as Clem Maxwell entered the room.

"Well, you boys have been up to mischief, haven't you?" he said in his Texas drawl. "I arrive to oversee the well renovation, and all I hear about is these crazy kids who almost got themselves killed, playing around under the rig.''

He stepped forward and briefly examined Joe's hurt leg. Satisfied that it wasn't serious, he straightened up. "You mind telling me what you were doing there?" he asked quietly.

Joe blinked and remembered Frank's telling him not to trust anyone. "I got lost," he said with a grin.

"Thanks, man," Dave Rubel said to Joe after Maxwell stalked out of the room. Frank stared thoughtfully after Maxwell, wondering what the man made of the Hardys' reticence. Frank hoped that Maxwell assumed they didn't want to talk in front of Rubel.

"No problem," Joe said, leaning back in his chair. "I figure we're more or less even now. So how about trading a little information?"

"Like what?" Rubel asked uneasily. "I already told you about Lopez."

"Like why you were spying on the standby boat," Joe suggested.

"I suspect they might be connected with Lopez somehow," Rubel snapped. "They might want to discredit Lone Star Oil so that a Mexican company can be brought in to finish."

"Joe thinks he saw someone signaling them from HomeBase last night," Frank said, glancing at Joe. "It was right before this well exploded. And we think the crew of the standby boat might be responsible for the broken underwater pipeline that was discovered by Deep Six.''

"But they couldn't have had anything to do with this cable accident, could they?" Joe demanded. "You were watching the boat right when it happened. They were too far away."

"Maybe the cable accident was just that—an accident," Frank suggested. "Maybe part of Lone Star's bad luck has been business as usual. That doesn't eliminate the standby boat's crew as suspects."

Rubel shook his head. "I'll get in touch with my people and see if they can check the crew out. Meanwhile," he added as he stood up, "I'd better go look like I'm doing some work. Are you going to wait here for the accident reports, Joe?"

"Right." Joe looked up at him, feeling pleased that Rubel was firmly on their side. "I think it might be a good idea if I stay out of trouble for a while."

"I'm due back at HomeBase," Frank said, rising. "You're sure you're okay, Joe?"

"Sure I'm sure. Get out of here," his brother said with a wave.

Frank crossed the platform, now swarming with men attempting to rethread the cable onto the hoist, and boarded his Bell 212. He fired up the chopper's engine, savoring the joy of the moment of liftoff. As he pulled away from the top of Delta rig's derrick, a familiar object came sailing into view on the surface of the ocean. The standby boat!

I might as well take a quick look while I'm here, Frank said to himself, impulsively changing the chopper's flight direction.

Under Frank's guidance, the Bell 212 swooped down over the small boat and hovered about fifty feet directly overhead. A group of crew members gathered on the deck, shielding their eyes from the powerful wind kicked up by the chopper's rotors. One of them, Frank noticed, was a young woman.

"Hmm," he said out loud. "Joe's right. She is good-looking."

There wasn't much more that Frank could see from that height, so he swung the chopper out over the waves in front of the boat. What could be stowed on a boat that size? Explosives, weapons, all sorts of tools for sabotaging an operation like Heron Field, he realized.

While he was pondering the situation, Frank's eyes happened to fall on the right side of the instrument panel.

"That's funny," he said, leaning forward for a closer look.

A red light was flashing on the panel, above the word *Oil*. Frank stared. The chopper's oil pressure was bottoming out!

Before he could think how to correct the situation, the chopper's engine began to sputter. Instinctively Frank grabbed the microphone.

"Mayday! Mayday!" he called. "This is Gamma

Delta 02! I have engine failure! Repeat, I have—"

Frank heard a last sputter, and then nothing more. The engine had cut out entirely, he realized, and the rotors had stopped turning. Frank's heart flew to his throat as the chopper hesitated in thin air, then began to drop like a bowling ball.

Frantic, Frank stared out the window at the water rushing up to meet him. Inside the chopper, there was nothing but deadly silence and the whine of the wind. Mayday was right, Frank realized with growing terror. This time, it wasn't a simulation!

# Chapter

## 13

FRANK WATCHED the Gulf of Mexico rush toward him like a gray wall. There was nothing he could do to stop the helicopter from its descent. The next instant the Bell 212 slammed into the ocean, the impact jerking Frank back and forth like a rag doll.

"Am I okay?" Frank was momentarily stunned by the crash, only dimly aware that his seat belt was digging painfully into his waist. Gradually he became aware that the seat belt had prevented him from sailing out of the pilot's seat, but he had been tossed to one side by the collision.

Coming to his senses, Frank struggled to sit up as the tiny craft bobbed wildly in the choppy sea. He peered through a spider web of cracks at the huge gray waves beating on the glass.

Grabbing his radio microphone, Frank called, "Mayday! Mayday! This is Gamma Delta! I have ditched in the ocean. Repeat! This is Gamma Delta."

"Roger," crackled Alvarez's voice over the speaker. "Are you all right, Lee?"

"Okay, I guess," Frank responded. "Fortunately, I was at a low altitude. It looks like the damage to the chopper is slight. She's not taking on any water yet, though this windscreen could give way at any minute."

"We read you," Alvarez responded. "We have a radar fix on your location. The standby boat, *Cinco de Mayo,* should be in your vicinity."

Frank chuckled wearily. "I know," he said. "I just about dropped down on them out of the sky. This is my first ditch at sea, sir. Please advise me on correct procedure."

"Get off the chopper before it sinks—that's correct procedure!" Alvarez barked.

Frank clutched a large orange life preserver as two hefty men hauled him out of the Gulf and onto the *Cinco de Mayo*'s windswept deck. Reaching the top, he thanked his rescuers and glanced back over his shoulder at his swamped chopper, listing in the restless sea.

"Are you all right?" Frank turned to see a beautiful young woman at his side. Her soft brown eyes and wavy brown hair made Frank breathe in sharply.

"Uh, yeah," he said. "Just fine."

"You *Americanos* fall into the ocean often," the woman mused, extending a hand for Frank to shake. "My name is Maria. Come on, we'll dry you off."

"I'm Frank Lee," Frank said, following her below. This was definitely the woman Joe had seen the night that the *Cinco de Mayo* picked him up. Now Frank could understand exactly why Joe didn't want to believe the crew was involved in any conspiracy. "Thanks for your help," he said to Maria. "I thought I was a goner there."

"You deserved to be!"

Frank stopped in his tracks. A large, stocky, black-haired man stood at the bottom of the stairs, his feet planted wide apart and his hands on his hips. He sneered disdainfully at Frank. "There's no way that helicopter will float until the rescue crew arrives," he said. "You obviously don't deserve to fly."

"The engines cut out," Frank defended himself. "The chopper ran out of oil. I checked it this morning, and the gauge read full!"

"Perhaps. But since the chopper will sink," the man said disdainfully, "I guess we'll never know."

"Hector!" Maria scolded. "Be quiet." She hesitated, then murmured, "More sabotage."

"That's right," Frank said. "That's what I think, anyway. Do you have any idea who might have done such a thing?"

Hector looked at Frank with anger in his eyes.

"No," he said. "But we know who will be held responsible. The Mexicans!"

"You're wrong," Frank said with conviction. "Not if they're innocent."

He felt a hand on his shoulder. It was Maria's. "Come on," the young woman said. "You'll catch cold out here. We'll find you a blanket."

Frank followed Maria into the boat's main cabin, where she removed a woolly blanket from a trunk. "Stay here," Maria said. "We'll pass HomeBase on our circuit of the field and drop you off."

After Maria left the cabin, Frank saw his chance. He crossed to a large wooden cabinet fixed to the far wall. Frank tried the doors—they were locked.

Moving toward a desk near the cabin door, Frank found navigational charts rolled up and stored in pigeonholes above the desk. He unrolled one and saw that it was a map of some of the fishing grounds off the Yucatán Peninsula. The next map he inspected showed the Bay of Campeche.

Quickly and efficiently, Frank spread a third map out on the desk. This one showed Heron Oil Field, with the four platforms and HomeBase clearly marked. The plan also showed the complex of pipelines beneath the rigs, illustrating how they merged to the main pipeline leading back to Mexico.

He was about to take out another chart when

the door opened. Frank spun around to see Maria entering the room.

"Are you lost?" she asked him with a puzzled smile.

"Well—yes, I guess," Frank improvised. "Actually, I was just curious about whether—well—whether there's something I should be looking for."

Maria's smile faded. Her features tightened as she closed the door behind her, and she straightened to her full height. "If you are talking about the *Cinco de Mayo*," she said in a sharp voice, "I can tell you that there is nothing to find here. We are merely a hired boat and crew. We are not responsible for any of the disasters that have happened on your rigs."

"What about the torn pipeline?" Frank pressed her. "Someone dragged an anchor over it last night. Who could have done it but you?"

Maria looked away from him. "The one who commits the act is not always guilty of the crime," she said mysteriously.

Frank tried to figure out what she meant, but her words didn't make sense. "What about Lopez?" he asked finally, grasping at straws. "Aren't you in contact with him?"

"Who is Lopez?" she asked sharply.

"Your signaler," Frank answered. "He was flashing signals to your boat last night, and he pushed a man overboard—the man you rescued!"

"Why would we have saved him if our 'accomplice' pushed him in?" Maria demanded quickly.

Then her eyes narrowed. "I don't like your questions," she said to Frank. "I think you should stay here until we return you to HomeBase."

With that, Maria left the cabin. Frank heard a lock on the door click into place. When he tried the door, it wouldn't open.

She has a point, Frank admitted to himself. Why would they save Joe from drowning if their own accomplice had tried to kill him? He gazed down at the chart of Heron Field on the desk, then took a closer look.

That's funny, Frank thought. When he and Joe had watched Blaine repairing the damaged pipeline, Deep Six had been off the southwest corner of Delta rig. This chart clearly showed the main pipeline off the northwest corner of the rig.

No wonder they damaged the pipeline with their anchor, Frank realized. Their chart was wrong!

Frank scanned the map for the signature of the man who had authorized it as accurate.

The name was Clem Maxwell.

## Chapter

# 14

"MAXWELL!" Frank suddenly realized that that name fit in with far too many of the mysteries surrounding Heron Field.

"Of course," Frank murmured. Who would have better access to the rigs than the man who was supposed to oversee them? He remembered the Deep Six skipper's description of Maxwell's anger when the skipper wanted to check the underground pipeline. He remembered the Texan's insistence that the rigs continue operating in spite of a hurricane forecast. And Maxwell was on Delta rig this afternoon when the cable broke, Frank reminded himself. The cable had almost killed or severely wounded Joe. Frank wondered if it was just coincidence, or whether Maxwell really was sabotaging the oil rigs and was afraid that the Hardys were on his trail.

But why would he want to sabotage the rigs? Frank wondered. Something didn't make sense— Maxwell had encouraged the boys' participation, insisting that they keep him posted on their progress. He had seemed so convincing when he railed against the terrorists for FOE. Had all that been a cover-up? Frank asked himself. It was still too early to tell.

Frank folded the chart into a small square to fit inside his damp jacket pocket. Then he glanced out a porthole at the churning sea.

The storm was approaching rapidly.

"Good job, kid," Thelma Hunnicut said to Joe, checking over the stacks of envelopes he had prepared. They contained boarding passes for every person in Heron Oil Field.

"You can call me Joe," he joked, but his mind was only half on the conversation. He was worried that the oil field would be evacuated before he could go through Hunnicut's files. He still needed to check employee descriptions and match them with Frank's attacker.

"Purdy, when do the Chinooks get here?" Hunnicut asked.

"Forty minutes and counting," he called out.

"Good. Take these passes to the helipad and prepare checkout tables. We're going to have to move everyone out double time. The storm will hit with full force in two hours, and we can't afford to panic."

"Gotcha," Purdy said as he left, carrying the envelopes.

"What's next?" Joe asked, hoping for time to have a go at the files.

"Most of the workers have returned to Home-Base, but a few are still securing the pumps on the fields," she said. "We're lucky things have run so smoothly today. Especially after losing one of the helicopters."

Joe's smile froze on his face. "We lost a helicopter?" he asked. "Which one?"

"Actually it was the one you took out to Delta rig. Luckily, the pilot escaped before the chopper sank."

"Is he all right?" Joe asked, trying to hide the anxiety in his voice.

"Oh, yeah, he's fine," said a familiar voice. Joe turned to see Frank standing in the doorway. "The *Cinco de Mayo* dropped me here," he said. "They're heading back to port."

"Good," Hunnicut said, giving Frank a wide, approving smile. "So—your first dive, huh, kid? How'd you like it?"

"Not bad, for a short swim," Frank said with an amused glance at his brother. "And, uh—you can call me Frank."

Hunnicut chuckled. "Blondie," she said, turning to Joe, "take him next door and get him an insurance form to fill out."

Joe started to correct her on his name again. Then he shrugged, giving up. "Aye aye, boss," he said instead, heading for the door.

"I'll see you two at the helipad in half an hour." Hunnicut stood and removed a huge ring of keys from her desk. "Meanwhile, I have some inventory to check on."

"Clem Maxwell?" Joe repeated, staring at his brother. "You really think he's responsible for the sabotage?" The Hardys were in Hunnicut's office, pulling files from the metal cabinets. "What could his motive be?"

"That's what we're looking for," Frank said. "Whose files do you have?"

"Purdy and Rubel," Joe said.

"And I have Lopez and Maxwell." Frank and his brother spread the files out on Thelma's desk. "Look for anything that could link them to the crimes," Frank said. "Criminal record, experience with explosives, computer expertise."

Joe nodded, and scanned the files' contents as quickly as he could. Any second now they'd hear the announcement to evacuate, and so far they hadn't found a thing.

"I know," Joe said, straightening up quickly. "We'll radio Dad. This constitutes enough of an emergency, don't you think? He should have more information now than we have in these files."

Moments later Fenton Hardy's voice came over the speaker. "Joe," he said, "is that you?"

"Yes, Dad," Joe replied. "I know you said not to call, but—"

"No, no. I'm glad you did. I understand the

field is about to be evacuated because of the hurricane.''

"Right," Joe said. "But, Dad, we've found some leads here. We wanted to know what information you have."

"Not much out of the ordinary," Fenton's voice crackled. "That Darryl Purdy seems to be a pretty sneaky character. He was accused of mail fraud once and embezzlement twice, but none of the charges ever stuck. Oh, and here's something," he added.

A roar of static interrupted Fenton's voice. "What?" shouted Joe. "I didn't hear you."

"I said it might not mean anything," Fenton's voice came faintly through the static, "but I researched the oil rig accident that involved the FOE terrorists. It turns out that two people at Heron Field also worked on that rig."

"Who, Dad?" Joe asked excitedly.

"Dave Rubel," he said. "And Clem Maxwell."

Frank leaned against Thelma Hunnicut's desk after Joe had ended the conversation with their father, pondering the news. "Two men are present at one offshore major disaster, and then show up at another oil field where it looks like a disaster's waiting to happen," he said. "What does it mean?"

"Maybe nothing," Joe said to his brother. "I'm surprised more people here didn't work on that rig. The pool of offshore oil workers can't be that big."

"Maybe, but I don't think so. There have been too many coincidences already." Deep in thought, Frank tapped his fingernails on the desktop. "What I do think, though, is that if that disaster's going to happen, it's going to happen very soon. If not, there won't be anyone here to appreciate it."

"What else could happen?" Joe asked. "I mean—I guess it could be anything. How can we know for sure?"

Suddenly Joe raised his head and stared at his brother. "Oh, no," he said, getting to his feet.

Frank met his gaze, bewildered. "What?" he said.

Without answering, Joe rushed to the steel door behind Thelma's desk. He grabbed the knob. It turned easily.

"Oh, no," he repeated with a groan.

"What is it?" Frank demanded, joining him.

"All of the explosives are gone!"

# Chapter

## 15

"NOW WHAT?" Joe stood stock still in front of the empty storeroom. "Do you think Maxwell actually plans to blow up the entire field?"

"I don't know," Frank replied. "But in theory, now would be the perfect time to do maximum damage. With the hurricane coming, everyone's busy securing the rigs and preparing to leave. A saboteur would have more freedom."

"But I still don't get it," Joe protested. "Why would a man whose livelihood depends on this oil field want to destroy it? Do you really think he had something to do with the Louisiana catastrophe, too?"

"I don't know," Frank snapped back, equally frustrated. "All I'm sure of is that your friend Maria is right—if push comes to shove, Lone Star is likely to blame the Mexican faction for any major damage. We'll have to catch Maxwell red-handed, or the wrong people are going to be accused."

"Who's going to be accused of what?" asked a stern voice. Thelma Hunnicut was standing in the doorway.

"There isn't time to give you the details, boss," Joe said. "But look—all the explosives are gone from the storage room. We're convinced that the saboteur who's been plaguing Heron Field is Clem Maxwell. We think he took the explosives and plans to blow up at least one of the rigs before we evacuate."

To Joe's great surprise, Hunnicut chuckled softly. "You've been reading too many detective stories, I think," she admonished him. "Clem Maxwell took the explosives, all right— and loaded them on the first Chinook helicopter that left for Houston. He insisted on seeing to that personally. We're not about to leave explosives lying around here during a hurricane."

"Did you actually see the explosives loaded onto the helicopter?" Frank asked.

Hunnicut frowned. "Well, no," she admitted. "But so what? It's not like Clem's going to hoard TNT in his cabin."

Joe exchanged a tense glance with his older brother.

"Come on," Frank said. "Let's find Maxwell and ask him."

\*　　\*　　\*

Frank led the way up to the deck of the flotel, with Joe and Thelma jogging behind. The wind had risen sharply and was now howling across the deck's surface. The sky was filled with swirling gray clouds, which were occasionally lit by massive forks of lightning.

"Wow," Frank murmured at the sight of two Chinook helicopters just lifting off the deck. Two more moved in to take their places and another pair hovered close by, waiting for their turn.

"Good," Thelma shouted from behind him. "The crowd's thinning. It looks like five or six choppers have already come and gone."

"There must be over a hundred guys still up here, though," Joe, joining Frank on deck, shouted over the noise of the wind and the rotors. Frank followed his gaze to the crowd lined up at a table behind the choppers where Darryl Purdy was handing out boarding passes.

Joe turned to his boss. "Where's Maxwell?"

"Would you forget Maxwell?" Thelma gave Frank an exasperated frown. "He has nothing to do with Lone Star's explosives!"

When Joe refused to back down, she sighed and shouted, "Okay, Blondie. Come on."

Excited, Joe and Frank hurried after Thelma as she strode across the deck to the flight control room.

"Alvarez," Frank heard her say as he entered the room behind Thelma. "Have you seen Maxwell?"

"Of course not," Alvarez said. "He's out of here—left on the first flight with the explosives, remember?"

"You saw him leave?" Frank asked sharply.

Alvarez seemed to be bewildered. "No, I—"

Frank exchanged a glance with Joe behind Thelma's back. "We'll be back in a minute," Frank said to Joe's boss as the Hardys headed for the door.

"Wait just a minute!" Thelma's imperious voice stopped the boys in their tracks. "Frank and Joe, enough of this nonsense. You need to pick up your boarding passes," she said. "All four of us are on the last flight out, and"—she peered around them through the half-open door— "it's leaving." She turned to Alvarez. "Come on, pal."

"I'm with you, Thelma." He turned back to the Hardys. "We'll see you in the chopper."

Stunned, Frank and Joe watched the pair leave. "What should we do?" Frank heard his brother ask. "Forget about Maxwell and save ourselves?"

"Come on," Frank said, heading toward the door. "I have an idea."

Once again, Frank found himself crossing the deck as a pair of Chinooks lifted off and the last pair began to drop down. Two lines of passengers had already formed, the workers impatient to get to safety. The sky had turned an eerie purplish gray, and the waves were as tall as a one-story building.

Frank arrived at the check-out table, where Darryl Purdy was beginning to shut things down. "About time you got here," he shouted over the noise. "Here are your boarding passes. Let's get out of here!"

"Wait a minute," said Frank. "Did Clem Maxwell pick up his pass?"

"What difference does that make now?" Purdy demanded. He grabbed the remaining passes off the table and started toward the choppers. "I don't know about you, but I'm leaving!"

"Let me see those," Joe said, snatching the boarding passes from him. Frank looked over his shoulder. There, in Joe's hand, was Clem Maxwell's unclaimed pass.

"And look," he heard Joe shout over the wind. "There are two more—one for Dave Rubel and one for Juan Lopez."

"Too bad!" Purdy yelled. "They had plenty of time to get out here."

"But what will happen to them?" Frank asked.

"How should I know? Anyway, that's their problem, isn't it?" Purdy rushed off to board one of the Chinooks.

Automatically, Frank and Joe followed the worker up to the chopper. Thelma Hunnicut's head appeared in the hatchway. "Are you coming or not?" she shouted at the boys.

Frank hesitated. "We can't leave the job unfinished."

"What job?" Hunnicut demanded. "Stupid paperwork? It can wait!"

Just then Frank heard the ring of a telephone, amplified over a speaker hanging over the control room door. "Wait a second!" he called to Thelma, and sprinted toward the control room.

With Joe close behind him, Frank raced into the control room and answered the phone that was ringing on the desk. "Hello?" he said, breathless.

"Thank goodness," he heard. "I thought everyone had cleared out!"

"Who is this!" Frank asked as Joe stood beside him, waiting impatiently.

"This is Rubel. Listen, there's no time for discussion. I'm on Charlie rig. Someone has opened up the main well here, and they've destroyed the automatic valves. Unless someone helps me shut this thing down, we're going to have the biggest oil spill in history!"

# Chapter

# 16

"IT'S MAXWELL," Frank said to Joe, hanging up the phone. "Come on."

Frank sprinted to the helipad, followed closely by his brother. "What's up?" Joe shouted as they reached the bottom of the ladder that led up to the Chinooks' cabin.

"That was Rubel," Frank told him. "Maxwell's at Charlie rig. We have to get over there, now."

"How?" Joe asked. The wind was howling even louder, and they could no longer hear Hunnicut's voice as she shouted at them from the hatch of the chopper.

"We'll take one of the Bells," Frank replied. "It won't take long, I hope. Then we can come back and get aboard the Chinook."

He turned toward Thelma Hunnicut and waved

131

her back into the cabin, holding up all ten fingers and pointing to his watch to signal that he needed ten minutes. He watched as Thelma tried to argue with him in pantomime, then gave up, shrugged elaborately and went inside. The hatch closed, and the chopper sat on the helipad, rotors spinning.

"I hope you know what you're doing, Frank," Joe shouted as he chased his brother toward the hangar. Frank waved dismissively over his shoulder, pulling open the hangar door and surveying the row of Bell 212s.

"Come on," Frank said, leading the way to the chopper nearest the door. He began undoing the leather straps that lashed down the rotors. Then, over the roar of the rising storm outside, he heard the rotors of the Chinook pick up speed.

"Hey!" Frank yelled, running to see what was going on. He arrived just in time to see the Chinook rise off the helipad, dip its nose, and shoot out over the sea.

"Purdy," he heard Joe scream from just behind him. "That weasel!"

"I guess he didn't want to wait around," Frank said. "He must have told the pilot to leave." Frank turned back toward the Bell 212, which looked a lot smaller all of a sudden.

"We're on our own, Joe," he said. "Let's get moving."

Frank sat behind the controls of the chopper, while Joe perched on the edge of the copilot's seat beside him. "Ready?" Frank heard his brother ask.

"Ready," Frank answered. He pressed the ignition. The engine of the small chopper roared to life; the rotors began to beat. Frank gently lifted the chopper a few inches off the floor of the hangar, and wheeled it around toward the door. The Bell skipped gracefully across the floor of the hangar and out into the howling storm.

"Okay, little brother," Frank said as they cleared the hangar. "This is it." He pulled back on the controls, sending the Bell into a steep climb. The swirling winds seemed to lift the small chopper into the pitch-black skies. As the chopper hovered high over HomeBase, Frank gazed down at the oil field spread out below them. The rigs were dark gray against the angry sea that beat against their pylons.

"Do you see anything?" Frank asked Joe. "Any movement or sign of life?"

"Nothing," Joe replied. "It's like a ghost town."

Frank turned the chopper toward the heart of the field and shot out over the water. The wind swirled, and as it struck the chopper from behind, Frank could feel the vehicle accelerate wildly.

Then without warning the chopper seemed to strike an invisible wall of air and moved forward only by inches. "The wind's fighting me," Frank told Joe, a knot forming in his stomach. It was as though a giant hand were trying to push them out of the sky.

This is just like the simulator, Frank realized as he fought the chopper's controls. Through a roar in his ears, he heard Joe cry, "Frank, what's wrong?"

They were losing altitude. Frank stared down at the churning whitecaps. Forcing himself not to pull back, risking a stall, Frank pressed forward on the controls and let the wind take them down and forward.

The chopper picked up speed and began to move forward at a far faster rate than they were dropping. "Frank!" Joe yelled as they skimmed just over the surface of the storm-tossed sea. A huge whitecap rose up in front of them, and the tiny Bell smashed through it. Frank pulled back on the controls, and the Bell came out of the dive.

Frank smiled at his brother. "You have to learn to roll with it, Joe," he said.

"*You* learn to roll with it." Joe was almost green.

Finally the chopper arrived at Charlie rig, and Frank just managed to land it on the helipad. As he switched off the engine, Frank saw Rubel sprinting toward the chopper.

"We have to hurry," he shouted to the Hardys. "Come on."

Rubel led the Hardys off the helipad and down a catwalk to a large steel building at the center of the platform. It must be the control room, where the drilling and pumping operations were coordinated, Frank realized. As they went inside, he spotted a bank of monitors and gauges against one wall. A white panel covered the other, filled with more gauges and switches.

"Wow," Joe said, examining a control panel near the door. "It looks like someone smashed it with a sledgehammer."

"That's nothing. Follow me," Rubel said, leading them out the back to a large metal shed.

Inside, Frank saw a dozen huge pipes rising out of the floor of the shed, each one about six feet tall and a foot thick. A large steel block with small wheel valves attached was affixed to the top of each pipe.

"Look at that," Frank said, pointing to the center pipe. The block on the pipe had been smashed up, and the wheel valves were sheared off.

"These pipes control the flow of oil from the wells," Rubel explained. "Someone's left the well wide open. Those electronic switches they destroyed inside the control room operate the well down on the ocean floor. And since the hand valves out here have been smashed, we can't close the pipe off manually."

"What *can* we do?" Joe asked.

"There's a safety valve below the deck," Rubel said. "It will pump water into the well, forcing the oil down into the seabed. If we get that open, we'll be all right—provided the rig isn't totally destroyed by the hurricane."

"We have to try," Frank said. "Let's go."

Rubel led the Hardys to a metal stairway leading below. It ended at a short catwalk. The pipes rose through the catwalk and the deck above. There were large circular valves, each about four feet across, attached to smaller pipes that fed into the main pipes. Frank spotted a set of huge monkey wrenches attached to the center pipe's valve.

"I tried opening it by myself," Rubel explained. "It wouldn't budge. I hope the three of us can do it."

Rubel took hold of one of the monkey wrenches, Frank and Joe the other. "On three," Rubel commanded. "One, two, three!"

Frank threw his weight against the wrenches along with the other two. He pushed so hard he felt as though the muscles in his arms would burst. Still, the valve didn't move.

"Again," Joe said. "On three."

Once again, they pushed in unison. The valve wouldn't budge, Frank realized. It was stuck—frozen. It—wouldn't—budge.

Frank sensed Joe tightening his grip, so he applied one extra ounce of strength—

The valve moved! Not much, Frank realized, but the valve's seal had been broken.

"We did it," Joe shouted. "Open her up!"

Together, they leaned into the valve one more time. This time, Frank felt the valve move a few inches under their combined strength.

A minute later Frank was gratified to see the

valve turning easily. He put his hand to the pipe. He could feel the vibrations of water rushing through and into the pipe that led to the well.

"We did it!" Joe said again.

"You certainly did," a familiar voice said. "Congratulations."

Frank turned toward the stairs and peered into the business end of a large handgun. On the other end stood Clem Maxwell. As Frank stared at him, he saw the chief operating officer's smile fill with menace.

# Chapter

# 17

"MAXWELL. I thought you might be behind this," snarled Rubel.

"Sure thing, Mr. Rubel. Thoughts are cheap, unfortunately."

"Give it up, Maxwell," Frank pleaded. "You can't go through with this. The hurricane—"

"The hurricane is perfect," Maxwell interrupted. "With its help I'm going to destroy FOE."

"And the Gulf of Mexico." Joe took a step toward the older man.

"Freeze right there," Maxwell ordered. "When they fish your bodies out of the water, I don't want them to find gunshot wounds, but I'll use this if I have to. Okay—march up the stairs," Maxwell ordered, stepping out of the way.

Joe started upstairs first, followed by Frank

and Rubel. Destroy FOE? Joe was thinking. Why does Maxwell want to destroy FOE? When he reached the deck he saw that the storm had increased. The wind howled now, and a pelting rain had begun to fall.

"Into the control room," Maxwell shouted above the storm. The three entered through the back door. "There's some cord in the cabinet," Maxwell said to Joe. "Frank, tie up Rubel and your brother."

While Joe and Rubel sat in chairs in front of the control panel, Frank got the cord from the cabinet. He began to wind the cord around Rubel.

"I had my eye on you, Maxwell," Rubel said. "All I needed was one piece of evidence."

"Evidence?" Maxwell asked in shocked surprise. "How about the lump on the back of this kid's head?"

"That was you!" Joe cried.

"Who else?" Maxwell drawled disdainfully.

"You must have pushed me overboard," Joe said.

"And you sabotaged my chopper!" Frank exclaimed.

"No hard feelings, I hope." Maxwell leaned against the wall. "I begged Baker not to send any detectives out here. I could handle the situation myself, I said. Well, it can't be helped now. At least your deaths will help to further discredit the so-called Federation of the Environment."

"I don't get it." Frank stood behind Joe's

chair, a length of cord in his hands. "You hate FOE, but you're the one trying to destroy this oil field. Why are you bankrupting the company you work for?"

"Ask this guy." Maxwell gestured with his gun at Dave Rubel. "Ask him if he remembers Beaumont Field ten years ago, almost to the day."

"Beaumont—" Rubel looked puzzled. "That's the oil field that was destroyed, right?"

"Don't play dumb with me, Rubel," Maxwell growled. "I know you were on that field when one of the rigs exploded. Everyone knows FOE planted that bomb. Do you remember how many people were killed? I'll tell you. Twenty-five."

"Yeah, I was there," Rubel said, "but I wasn't a member of FOE back then. I was just maintaining equipment. I didn't know FOE existed."

"I bet." Joe watched the barrel of Maxwell's gun tremble as it pointed at Rubel. "Well, I'll tell you something, Rubel," he said. "Even if that's true, it doesn't matter. I'm out to pin this sabotage on FOE, and if you get hurt in the process, so be it. Your bunch isn't going to get away with murder this time."

"But why?" Joe interjected. "What grudge do you have against FOE?"

Maxwell looked at Joe, his eyes vague and glassy. "I had a son once," he said. "He wanted to grow up to be just like his daddy—working on the offshore rigs just like me. That boy was the joy of my life, until—''

Maxwell's voice broke. Joe eyed the gun, which trembled violently. ''Until what?''

''He went out on his first job with me ten years ago.'' Maxwell spat out the words with difficulty. ''It was Beaumont Field. He was so excited—he was only seventeen.''

''I don't remember you there—'' Rubel said.

''Shut up!'' The gun swung back to Rubel. ''I was there,'' Maxwell assured him. ''I didn't recognize you at first, either, when you signed on at Heron. But I happened to check out your employment record, and then I remembered.''

''Did your son— Was he—'' Frank asked hesitantly.

Maxwell nodded. ''One of the twenty-five, blasted into the sky from the force of the bomb. We never found even a piece of his clothing to bury.''

There was silence in the control room. Maxwell took a deep breath and removed a key from his pocket. ''See this?'' he said, holding it up to the trio.

''My office key?'' Joe ventured.

''Right.'' Maxwell shoved the key into Rubel's pants pocket.

''What's that for?'' Rubel demanded. Joe noticed that a cold sweat had broken out on Rubel's forehead.

''It's the final, conclusive evidence of your guilt,'' Maxwell said. ''Now everyone will assume you were the one who stole this young man's key. Then, in the confusion of the evacuation, you used it to break into Thelma's office and steal the explosives."

Joe made a move for Maxwell, but the Texan responded instantly by cocking his gun at Joe's head.

"Don't try it, boy," Maxwell said, his eyes bulging. "I've got no way out now but with this."

"You're nuts!" Joe yelled.

"Why, because I plan to blow up this rig in the middle of a hurricane and cause an oil spill that will make Beaumont look like a case of bathtub ring?" Maxwell chuckled softly and waved his gun in Frank's direction. "Tie him up, like I told you to—or else."

Frank caught Joe's eye as he began to tie his brother's arms behind his body. Joe nodded imperceptibly, then tensed his arm muscles as Frank tied him up. When Joe relaxed his muscles, the cord binding him would be loose.

Meanwhile, Maxwell leaned over Rubel. "How does it feel, son?" he taunted, his eyes blazing with hatred. "Are you scared to die?"

"I didn't do anything to your son," Rubel said, trembling. "You're punishing the wrong person!"

"I bet you feel like my son felt ten years ago," Maxwell continued, ignoring the man. "Imagine what it was like to have the rig he was standing on explode in a ball of fire. Think about my son, Rubel!"

"FOE was wrong back then. But, please, stop this insanity. There's too much at stake."

"I know what's at stake." Maxwell glanced at his watch. "In four minutes a bomb will go off on Charlie rig, turning this platform into a heap of twisted metal. FOE will be the obvious culprit, and my son will have his revenge."

Maxwell tucked his gun under his belt and began tying Frank up.

"Thanks for stopping by with that chopper," he said. "It gives me a fighting chance of getting to the next rig. I wasn't looking forward to swimming. In fact, you probably saved my life."

Drawing the cord painfully tight around Frank's wrists, he secured the knots. "I'll tell your daddy you boys died like heroes, while I wasted time looking for you on the wrong rig."

While Maxwell was busy with Frank, Joe had relaxed his muscles and was slowly working his wrists free. Now he watched Maxwell closely, waiting for the moment to make his move.

Just then Joe heard a clatter outside the control room. Maxwell drew the gun from his belt and stepped to the door.

A hand lashed out from the side of the deck and knocked the gun from Maxwell's hand.

"Lopez!" Joe shouted as the attacker came into view. Joe worked his arms frantically against the cords that bound them, as Lopez swung a roundhouse punch to Maxwell's jaw, staggering him.

"Hurry!" Joe heard Frank mutter. Joe worked his arms up and down while he watched Maxwell regain his balance, then grab something from his left boot. Joe saw the object glint in the light. It was a switchblade.

"Joe, now's your chance!" Frank said frantically.

"You shouldn't have done such a good job tying me!" Joe responded as he worked against the cords. On the deck, he saw Maxwell brandish the knife as Lopez circled him. Maxwell lunged; Lopez stepped nimbly aside and grasped Maxwell's wrist. He twisted around and brought Maxwell's arm down on his knee. Maxwell screamed, dropped the knife, and fell to his knees.

Suddenly Joe's left arm sprang free of the restraints. He yanked the cords from his hands and ran onto the deck to help Lopez.

The skies opened. What had been a driving rain now became a sheet of water. Joe peered through the storm to see Lopez and Maxwell locked in each other's arms. They were staggering toward the center of the rig directly beneath the main derrick.

"Maxwell!" Joe screamed, but neither Maxwell nor Lopez could hear him through the storm.

Joe watched in horror as the two men disappeared, falling through the central hole in the platform. Joe sprinted through the rain and wind to the edge of the hole and peered over, but saw nothing but the churning, windswept waves far below.

"They're gone!" Joe sprinted back toward the control room. He picked up Maxwell's knife and used it to free Rubel and Frank. "They fell through the center of the rig and washed out to sea!"

"We'll be gone, too, in a few minutes, unless we hurry," Frank said, rubbing his wrists. "That bomb is probably directly beneath us, on the concrete pylons supporting the pipes. That's where it would do maximum damage."

"What should we do?" Rubel said, starting to panic.

"I know something about explosives," Frank told him. "I'll defuse it."

"Okay," Rubel said. "We'll use this cord as a safety line. Tie it around your waist. Joe, you go under the platform with him. You know your way around by now. I'll anchor you both up top."

The three raced out into the driving storm, waves crashing. Joe tied one end of the cord around his waist, the other end around Frank's waist. Twenty feet of cord stretched between them.

"There's a ladder in the corner," Rubel called over the howling wind. "See if the bomb's there."

"Right," Frank shouted. He crossed to the ladder and began descending it. Joe noticed how wet and slick the rungs were and flinched when Frank nearly lost his footing. Joe took a deep breath and followed him down.

As he descended, Joe could see that the ladder was attached to the concrete pylon that supported the center of the rig. Forty feet below deck, the ladder passed by some scaffolding. Below Joe, Frank reached the walkway and began searching for the bomb.

Joe stopped on the ladder, looking down past the metal pipes at the storm-tossed waves that washed higher and higher. Then his eye was caught by a shoe box–size lump wedged between one of the pipes and the concrete pylon. "Frank," Joe called. "There!"

Looking closer, Joe could see that the lump was made of something that looked like Play-Doh. A large battery and an egg timer were bound to it with electrician's tape. Wires passed from the battery to the timer, and from the timer into the plastic.

"Hand me the knife," Frank shouted over the roar. Joe handed him Maxwell's switchblade. Frank crawled onto the scaffolding. Huge waves licked its underside as Frank got down on his belly. Joe watched his brother lean over the scaffolding to touch the bomb.

It was just out of his reach, Joe realized. As he watched helplessly, Frank inched closer. A wave washed over the walkway, nearly pushing him off.

"How much longer do we have?" Joe shouted.

"Thirty seconds," Frank yelled back.

Another wave washed over the scaffolding, and Frank was forced to hold on tight until it had passed. Then he brushed the water from his eyes and examined the wiring. A penny was taped to the timer. At zero hour, Frank realized, the penny would complete the circuit on the battery and the bomb would explode.

Frank checked the timer. Fifteen seconds!

Opening the switchblade, he stretched as far as he could toward the bomb. The tip of the knife came just short of the wire that led from the battery to the timer. Frank twisted his body to get a bit more reach. His shoulder was beginning to go numb.

This time the tip of the blade barely nosed under the wire. Frank pushed up with the knife, straining every fiber in his body.

The wire came free! Frank almost lost his balance with the sudden motion, and he made a grab at the scaffolding. Then he almost fell again as the timer went off, its buzz echoing loudly.

"That was close." Frank rolled over on his back and lay panting. Above him, Joe grinned and gave him the thumbs-up sign. An instant later, though, Frank saw Joe's smile turn to a look of horror.

"Frank! Watch out!" he screamed.

It was too late. A huge wave crashed over the scaffolding, engulfing Frank. Flailing wildly, Frank felt himself lifted up and carried away, helpless against the awesome power of the ocean.

As the wave receded, the pylon was stripped bare, except for the pipes running up it from the ocean floor to the platform. There was no longer any bomb, or scaffolding, or ladder.

There were no longer any Frank and Joe Hardy.

# Chapter

# 18

JOE HARDY burst up out of the ocean, salt water spewing from his mouth. High, crashing waves beat his head and upper body, but he was able to kick his legs and keep his head above water. He strained his neck to see over the tops of the waves, and realized that he'd been washed almost a hundred feet from the ladder. Rubel was nowhere in sight at the edge of the gap in the platform. Where was Frank?

"Frank!" Joe yelled, though he knew the howling wind would swallow his voice.

Joe tugged on the rope still wrapped around his waist. To his relief, it went taut. Frank was still tied to the other end! His heart pounding, Joe began to pull the rope in. Frank's head was bobbing above the waves about fifteen feet away. With four mighty tugs, Joe brought his brother next to him.

"Frank," called Joe. "Are you okay?"

Frank was conscious. Joe watched as his older brother spit out water and tried to talk. All Frank could do was nod his head to let his brother know he was alive and able to swim.

"Let's head for that corner pylon," Joe shouted. "There's a ladder that leads up to the deck." Joe and Frank began swimming in that direction.

As they approached the pylon, Joe saw something that made his heart leap. There, moored to a large iron ring, was the *Cinco de Mayo!* He patted Frank's shoulder and pointed to the boat. Then he continued swimming with renewed vigor.

It was easier than Joe had thought to reach the *Cinco de Mayo.* The force of the waves helped carry the Hardys there. When they were about forty yards away, Joe began yelling for help, but he was still too far to be heard.

"Come on, Frank," Joe muttered, swimming hard. "Not much farther." He gathered his brother under his arm and performed the lifesaver's crawl stroke toward the boat. As he got nearer, he called again.

A figure appeared on deck, and Joe heard a voice holler to them from across the waves. Joe yelled back and tugged his brother closer to the boat. When he was within twenty yards, Joe saw the standby boat's familiar-looking orange life saver splash into the water a few feet away.

"We made it," Joe shouted to Frank as he grasped the ring life saver. He relaxed the rest of his body as a firm hand began to haul the two Hardys onto the boat.

Joe heard voices speaking in Spanish as he and Frank reached the hull. A pair of strong hands grabbed Joe under the arms and pulled him up the rest of the way. He fell in a heap on the deck and watched as the men pulled Frank up behind him. A gentle hand touched the back of Joe's neck.

Joe stared up into a pair of shining brown eyes. "Are you all right?" Maria asked him.

Joe smiled weakly. "We've got to stop meeting like this," he said.

The sky was a brilliant blue, and the warm sun bathed the deck of HomeBase. Joe Hardy grinned as Dudley Baker patted him proudly on the back. Fenton, Frank, and Dave Rubel were there. Dave had been taken on board the *Cinco de Mayo* along with Lopez who had swum to it when he fell into the ocean.

"You saved more than just an oilfield, son," Baker said to Joe.

"That's for sure," Joe agreed. "I saved Frank, too."

The others laughed. Then the smile vanished from Baker's face as he saw Maria and Lopez emerge on deck.

"These are the people you were telling us about?" Baker asked the Hardys.

"Yes," said Frank. "They had no intention of

sabotaging the rig—just the opposite. They saved our lives more than once."

Maria and Lopez approached the group tentatively. "You asked to speak to us, sir?" Lopez asked Mr. Baker.

"Yes, sir, I did." Baker extended a hand toward Lopez. "I believe we owe you an apology, Mr. Lopez," he said as the two shook hands.

Juan Lopez stiffened. "Don't apologize to me," he said. "Apologize to the Mexican Petroleum Workers Union. We heard the rumors of sabotage on the rigs. We were afraid that enemies among the American workers would destroy the rigs and lay the blame on us. It would have ruined our union."

As he spoke, Joe noticed Maria, who was even more beautiful in the bright light.

"Funny," Joe said to her, "I never would have figured you for an oil workers' rep."

Maria blushed slightly and laughed.

"Maybe once we're back on shore you could tell me how you got involved in that line of work," Joe suggested, moving closer. "And after that, we could go to a movie."

Maria's eyes sparkled as she smiled at the younger Hardy. "I can tell you the whole story now, Joe. It's very simple."

She slipped an arm around Lopez's waist. "You see, Juan is my husband. We have always worked side by side on everything."

"Your husband?" Joe blushed and backed off a step. Lopez, Frank, and Fenton laughed.

"I've been meaning to ask you, Mr. Lopez," Frank said, deciding to ease Joe's embarrassment, "why were you signaling the standby boat that night?"

"It was my way of letting them know if I had found any clues to the saboteur's identity," Lopez told him. "We hoped to catch him ourselves, to prove our innocence, but you boys beat us to it."

"Juan signaled once a week," Maria told Frank. "We would bring the boat nearby, and he would toss a message overboard. It was a simple system, but it worked."

Fenton Hardy shook his head. "I confess, even when I discovered that Clem Maxwell was present at Beaumont Oil Field, I never suspected he was behind this. Are you sure he drowned?"

"They found his body early this morning. Apparently, his wrist was broken in his fight with Lopez, so he couldn't swim."

"I started suspecting him when he seemed to show up before or after every so-called accident," Rubel put in. "But I didn't remember him from Beaumont Field. And I never knew about his son."

"Yes, it's sad," Baker said, shaking his head. "Maxwell was a good man. His son's death caused something to snap inside, I guess."

A silence fell upon the group, but it was soon

interrupted by a ruckus erupting behind them. Joe turned to see Thelma Hunnicut climbing up the ladder to the deck, with an abashed Darryl Purdy behind her.

"Go on, Purdy," Hunnicut barked. "Apologize to these boys!"

"Yeah," Joe said. "What was the big idea, abandoning us like that?" He glanced at Lopez. "To say nothing about the way you treated half the other workers on this field."

"Okay, okay." Purdy scowled at the ground as though he'd just tasted something he didn't like. "Frank and Joe," he recited in a monotonous voice, "I'm sorry I ordered the Chinook to leave without you. I just panicked, that's all. I thought we were going to be struck by lightning."

Then he muttered sulkily, "The hurricane bypassed the rigs, anyway. It's not like you were in any big danger."

"And the rest?" Joe demanded, not relenting at all.

Purdy looked up at him, then glanced over at Lopez. Lopez waited impatiently, with Maria at his side.

"Fine," Purdy said, sticking out a hand to Lopez. "I apologize. I know I said a lot of bad things to you guys. I really did think you were responsible for all that was going wrong."

"Maybe next time you'll look around for evidence before you blame whole groups of people for crimes they didn't commit," Lopez replied. Then, grudgingly, he shook Purdy's hand.

"Fine, fine!" Baker said, slapping a hand on each man's shoulder. "That's better. Actually, I'd say this entire operation is beginning to look up. Starting tomorrow, I'm going to step up production."

He looked at Joe as if a new idea had struck him. "That means we'll need more oil men. Joe, would you and Frank like to sign up for another shift?"

"With all due respect, sir, not on your life," Joe responded with a grin. "Thanksgiving Day is the day after tomorrow, and I haven't started on my tan yet."

"You can work on your tan on an oil rig, son," Fenton said, smiling.

"Maybe so, Dad," Joe said, tossing an arm around his brother's shoulders. "Call me old-fashioned, but for some reason, I prefer to do my work lying on a nice, solid beach!"

# Frank and Joe's next case:

Mark Stevens is America's king of horror writers, but now someone is trying to knock him off the throne. He's invited two of his biggest fans, Frank and Joe Hardy, into his home—Nightmare House—to investigate a bizarre series of threats against his life. The strangest twist of all is that in finishing his new book, Stevens may have written his own obituary!

The writer faces his worst nightmare—the terrors of his imagination have come to life. Evil poltergeists, deadly poisons, and razor-sharp guillotines have risen from the novel's pages to torment Stevens in his own home. If Frank and Joe don't find a way to demolish the plot and defuse the danger, the last chapter could be murder . . . in *Real Horror*, Case #71 in The Hardy Boys Casefiles™.